THE FIGHTING TEXAN

Jim Quartermain was a lean, hard, tough Texan. On the surface, the only difference between him and all the other men in town was the 75¢-worth of tin he wore on his chest. But to Jim Quartermain, that tin star was something only the undertaker would get away from him.

Then one night something happened that made Jim Quartermain rip off the star, and head out looking for people to kill . . .

THE FIGHTING TEXAN

Will Cook

GUNSMOKE

First published in the UK by Hale

This hardback edition 2008
by BBC Audiobooks Ltd
by arrangement with
Golden West Literary Agency

ISBN 978 1 405 68194 0

British Library Cataloguing in Publication Data available.

Printed and bound in Great Britain by
Antony Rowe Ltd., Chippenham, Wiltshire

FOREWORD

At the close of the Civil War, there came to the West a new breed of men, the gunfighters. Because Texas was their home, they returned and fathered a new era, the era of the fast-draw, two-gun technique. An outstanding leader in this school was Cullen Baker, ex-guerrilla, outlaw, and master of the gunfighters until his death in 1869.

There were other men who ranked with Baker. Ben Bickerstaff, Bob Lee, Bill Longley, Jack English, Joel McKitrich . . . . Some of these men were little more than killers, while others did not kill at all, but passed on the magic in their hands to other men who did. This is not a story of the master. It is the story of a pupil who learned too well.

WILL COOK

CHAPTER 1

River Street ran north and south through Crystal City, and during the hours of darkness Jim Quartermain walked this street alone, meeting its violence with violence, presenting a stubborn-willed front of law to the lawless. Quartermain was not a big man, or an impressive one. He did not shout or strike out often, for by nature he was a silent man who got his way by the never-ending small pressures he brought to play against the toughness of River Street.

Every evening at seven he would emerge from the hotel in a dark suit and high crowned hat. Every morning at seven when his nightly stint was finished, he would have his coffee and sausages at Rita Donegan's restaurant, saddle his horse and ride from town.

His ranch lay in a valley three miles from Crystal City. Trees lined the wagon road leading to it and within the nine hundred and sixty acres embraced by fence, there stood a white, two-story house and a large red barn. Bunkhouse and cookshack were set off from the house to the north, while several other small outbuildings clustered behind the barn. In the yard there was a well with a stone curb and a peaked roof over it.

Pausing by the hitch-rack near the wide front porch, Jim Quartermain sat his saddle and looked around. There was no sign of habitation on this ranch designed for easy living. No cattle grazed in the valley and no horses milled in the pole corral. The bunkhouse had never known an inhabitant, for no one lived here.

Dismounting, Jim Quartermain tied his horse and went inside, closing the screen door softly behind him. This was summer and the ripe flavors of hot earth filled the air and a bluejay called from the cottonwoods shading the west side of the house.

7

The interior was neatly in order, for a woman came from Crystal City once a week and cleaned everything. Curtains hung over the windows and book-lined shelves bracketed the fireplace. Selecting a soft chair, Jim Quartermain settled himself, extracted a cigar from a glass humidor, and spent several careful minutes preparing it for the match.

There were these hints of the perfectionist in Jim Quartermain's manner. He wasted no motion. He moved only when he was certain that movement would produce the desired results. Methodically, he attempted to remove all improbables from the equations of his life.

He was still a young man, twenty-seven or so, but surprisingly serious. As a rule he did not laugh often, but there was no surliness about him. Neither was he a sad man for there was none of this in his eyes or in the relaxed set of his lip half-hidden by his mustache. Quartermain was a man fine drawn by the guarded habits of his life, a man who was as familiar with the seamy side as he was with the more genteel.

On the small table by his chair sat a mahogany box, fat at the base and tapering toward the top. A small door was hinged and hooked on the front and a winding key protruded from the back. Leaning forward in his chair, Quartermain opened the front and pulled out the raised and weighted wand, and when he wound the mechanism, the wand ticked back and forth in measured cadence. By raising or lowering the metronome weight, Quartermain could slow or speed up the beat.

Leaving his chair, he crossed to a closed desk in the corner and slid up the roll top. A gun and holster lay there and he buckled the belt around his waist, settling the gun on his hip. After spinning the cylinder to make sure the gun was empty, he replaced it in the holster and began to time himself with the metronome.

He drew the gun on a mental impulse and rapidly produced a series of dry clicks by fanning the hammer. Then he slid the small weight down on the wand, increased the speed slightly, and repeated the entire process.

Ben Bickerstaff had taught him to do this. Bickerstaff and Lee, of Texas. Drawing a gun with furious speed was merely a matter of completely controlling the reflexes until the draw could be measured in fractions of a second. But the question arose as how those fractions would be

8

measured, or even guessed at with any degree of accuracy.

So Bickerstaff began using the musician's metronome, set for sixty clicks a minute, or double that. A man who could draw and click the hammer once was getting his shot off in a theoretical half-second. But Jim Quartermain was better than Bickerstaff. He got his shot off regularly in half that time. One quarter of a second for the draw and shot.

Almost as good as Lee, he decided, and went on practicing.

After a half hour of this he left the house, crossed the yard and went behind the barn. Along the west wall a bunker of old railroad ties had been erected and before this stood a wooden rack. Cracked beer mugs and empty whiskey bottles were stacked to one side.

Quartermain placed six of the beer mugs on the rack, spacing them a foot apart, then walked away from the bunker until twenty feet separated him from them. He let his arms dangle loosely at his sides, the portion of his right forearm between wrist and elbow lightly touching the stag handle of his sawed-off Remington.

Then Jim Quartermain drew and fired.

His speed was well under half a second. The muzzle tilted sharply from the recoil and glass flew in a bright shower of fragments. Shoving the gun into the holster, he stepped back one pace and drew again. At the last shot, he marked the spot with a wiping motion of his toe in the dust and went to the bunker to sweep off the broken glass.

With the gun reloaded, Jim Quartermain picked up a beer mug, tossed it high, then drew. He followed it for a split second as he sighted along the barrel. Then the gun bucked and the glass slivered in a bright spray.

Taking two mugs with his left hand, he threw them together, drawing the .44-40 as they separated. He fired while they were still climbing, shattering one. He cocked quickly and caught the other three feet off the ground.

Replacing the spent shells, he stood in the strong sunlight and looked at the gun in his hand. The 1875 Remington had been reworked by a clever gunsmith. The seven and a half inch barrel had been shortened by two inches until it came to the end of the ejector rod web. The hammer had been flattened where the thumb normally gripped it and the trigger was drilled and fastened back against the guard with a machine screw. The weapon of a gunfighter, fast, balanced, reliable.

Quartermain shoved it into his holster and picked up four whiskey bottles and placed them so that they formed a square thirty feet across.

Stationing himself in the exact center, he drew, breaking the two bottles in front of him before whirling to shatter the two behind. He broke the four bottles in slightly more than two seconds, using the thumb of his left hand to work the hammer.

With gun in hand, Jim Quartermain walked back to the house and spent twenty minutes cleaning his pistol. After he had removed all trace of the powder, he replaced it in the desk and rolled the top down again. From the road the distinct rattle of a buggy drew nearer and he went outside to the porch.

The buggy wheeled into the yard and Quartermain stepped down, smiling now. He handed a young woman to the ground while she gave him a warm smile and raised both hands to reseat her wide hat with dangling plume. Quartermain said, "This is a pleasant surprise, Carrie."

He took her arm and they walked to the cool shade of the porch.

Carrie Holderman was tall and somewhat slender, at first glance. When she removed her hat, hair fell to her shoulders in a brown cascade. She had a rounded body and her dress rustled softly as she moved past Jim Quartermain to enter the house. She stood for a moment in the hall, looking around.

"I never tire of coming here," she said, and moved into the parlor, tossing her hat onto a low stool as she stripped off her gloves. "I seem to feel more at home here than any place else." She looked at him quickly. "Is that wrong, Jim? Admitting that?"

A smile moved into his eyes. "Not wrong, Carrie. Just confusing."

Carrie's eyes were pale and darting and missed nothing as they flicked over the room. She moved toward his chair and ran her hand across the back, canting her head sideways when she saw the metronome. The spring had unwound and the wand had stopped. She touched it idly with her finger, watched it oscillate for a moment and then stop.

10

"Practicing? It's too hot out."

"Heat is relative," Quartermain said. "The nights are cool, but I've found it hot as hell on River Street."

"That's a poor joke," she said, and lifted the metronome, closing the cover before replacing it on the small table. "I heard the shooting on the way from town. Did you miss?"

"No," Quartermain said.

Carrie turned to him, her eyes grave. "Why is it so important, Jim? Do you have to miss?"

"It's human to make mistakes," he said. "I consider them the marks of normalcy." His seriousness vanished and he smiled. "Care for some cool beer?"

For a moment she see-sawed between her curiosity and his hint to let the subject drop. "All right. I love beer, although drinking it will make me fat."

They went into the kitchen and Quartermain raised the cooler while she seated herself at the table. He poured a glass for her, scraped off the head with a knife, then poured his own and sat down across from her. She drank and put the glass down. Foam made a pale mustache on her upper lip and she laughed and wiped it off.

"I'm in love with this place," Carrie said, looking around the kitchen. Dishes hung on hooks in a glass paneled cupboard. White curtains filtered the harshness from the streaming sunlight. "I've always had the notion you were thinking of a woman when you had this built, Jim. And there have been times when I've been terribly jealous of her. She must have had a great influence on your thinking."

"There was no woman," Quartermain said, and hooked his arm over the back of his chair.

Carrie Holderman regarded him seriously for a moment, then said, "Then why did you build it, Jim?"

"I needed it," Quartermain said. "A man has to build something or his life is nothing." His brows drew down and slight lines appeared around his eyes. "I learned my trade from one of the best, Carrie—Lee of Texas. But I don't want to end up as he did, with a tired horse and a ten dollar watch and a used pistol. I've got to have something solid behind me. Some reason for just being alive."

"Does the house make the difference?"

He moved his shoulders restlessly. "In a way, I think it does." He leaned forward, his elbows on the oilcloth cover. "A man doesn't really know much about himself—

11

why he is what he is, or what makes him different from other men. Life's a search, Carrie, and when a man finds the answers he's complete. I'm not complete."

"But what answers are there?" she asked. She reached across the table to put her hand over his. "You're an educated man, Jim. You know you can't build a house as a shrine to a security you don't have. Give up River Street. Live here and you'll find the answers."

"I like your voice," he said softly. "It's a very pretty voice. But you're just talking words, Carrie. I walk River Street and I own it, but that's not enough for me. A man can't live in the dirt without getting some of it on him. Back home in Texas I knew the old bunch, Carrie, the top guns, and I made the mistake of learning too much. I shot a man there, in the San Saba. Afterward, I was sorry, but there was no other way but to shoot. Later, I had to shoot another and then I found out what the others must have known all along, that each time it gets easier. That's what I have to fight, Carrie. I don't want to be like Baker or Longley."

"Or like Bob Lee?"

"Lee was different," Quartermain said. "The trouble was, a lot of men knew he was fast and wouldn't leave him alone."

Her hand tightened on his and her voice pleaded. "Jim, just give it up. Put the gun down and forget you ever carried one. You told me about your friend, McKitrich. He was going to do that."

Quartermain shook his head. "Joel said he was, but that's a long way from doing it. I'd be like a drunk who's swore off whiskey, Carrie. Every time a man crossed me I'd have to fight myself. When I put it aside it will be because there's no further need for it in my life." He sipped his beer, a troubled man who was in the habit of keeping it to himself. "I *am* like Lee and it worries me. He was fast, Carrie—the fastest I ever saw. The word spreads quick on a man like that." He smiled. "It's spread on me. Too many men who have come and gone in Crystal City. Too many men who remember me."

She possessed a great love for him; he could read it in her eyes. "Jim, why do you make me say it all the time? Isn't there anything in your heart for me?"

He patted her hand and then withdrew his own. "Don't

12

say it, Carrie. We like each other and we'd better leave it that way. Some day it might be different, but right now it isn't."

"Of course," she said, and got up, replacing her chair neatly. Her smile was forced and this bothered Jim Quartermain for she was a gay girl with laughter always near the surface.

When she stepped toward the hall door he took her arm and said, "Do you have to go, Carrie?"

"Do you really want me to stay?" She gave him a troubled smile. "Let's not pretend with each other, Jim. Neither of us do it well enough to get by."

He said no more until they reached the waiting buggy. "Carrie, what's the matter with me?"

"I don't think anything is," she said seriously. "Only you don't believe that."

A smile broke the solemnity of his face and his touch on her bare arms was light. Her lips changed faintly, becoming more full and inviting, and he pulled her against him and kissed her. In spite of his discipline, his emotions broke through and he became demanding.

When he released her, a new smile was curving her lips and deep pleasure tinted her voice when she said, "I can wait a while longer now. You've told me what I wanted to know."

Placing his hands on the softness above her rounded hips, he lifted her into the rig. She settled in the seat and picked up the reins. "You'll come to supper, won't you?"

"Yes," he said, and watched her drive from the yard. When he could no longer see her through the trees flanking the road, he went back into the house, slamming the screen door behind him.

CHAPTER 2

For an hour Jim Quartermain lay back in his deep chair, his feet cocked on a wide footstool. With the curtains drawn across the front windows, a dimness made the room cool, and he slept.

When a knock rattled the front door, he came awake immediately and went to see who it was. The sun was almost vertical now and the heat remained thick like a stain on the land. The yard was dry and crusted like a cracked scab and sundogs danced farther down the valley.

Judge Enright came in when Quartermain opened the door. Enright was a portly man, fifty some, with hair shot with gray. His face was florid, a blend of good whiskey and the heat.

"Bad news," he said. "Kurt Harlow bailed Slimmie out of jail less than an hour ago."

"Didn't you think he would?" Quartermain asked. He motioned the judge into the parlor and when Enright sat down, Quartermain went into the kitchen for more beer. He handed Enright the glass and the judge drank deeply. After wiping the foam from his mustache, he said, "Jim, you worry the hell out of me sometimes."

Quartermain laughed and settled in his chair. He rekindled a dead cigar and said, "Winn hates like hell to give up, Harry. You ought to know that better than I do." He moved the cigar from one side of his mouth to the other with a series of visings of his jaws.

"Winn wants you dead," Enright said flatly. "Don't you give a damn?"

"Sure," Quartermain said, "but sometimes I wonder if you do. Or anyone else in Crystal City, for that matter."

"Men hire the law then wash their hands of it," Enright insisted. He glanced at the marshal from beneath brows that were thick and unruly. "The problem is Winn Harlow and what to do about him. He wants Main as well as River Street and he means to get it."

"Not while I'm city marshal," Quartermain said, "and he knows that too."

The judge sighed heavily and patted his pockets for a cigar. Jim Quartermain offered him one from the humidor and Enright popped a match on his shoe sole. "You're only one man, Jim. One gun. Winn has pulled a fast one on you this time and he'll wait for you tonight."

"I intend to meet him," Quartermain said. "Are you worried, Harry?"

"Dammit, yes!" Enright snapped. "You called this showdown on Winn and he accepted it: twenty-four hours to clear out of town. But then he turned around and

14

gave you twelve to do the same. That twelve hours is up tonight at seven." Leaning forward in his chair, Enright held his cigar clamped tightly between his teeth. "The toughs that pass through here are getting cautious with you, Jim. You don't miss when you shoot and it worries the hell out of them. The odds are getting too steep from the front so they'll start evening them up from the back. Maybe that's why Winn bailed Slimmie out, to wait in an alley."

"Tonight we'll find out," Quartermain said quietly. "Winn must think he can beat me, Harry. He's a cautious man and likes the odds in his favor."

"Slimmie is his odds," Harry Enright insisted. "Dollars to nothing if you take care of Slimmie first, Winn'll run."

"There's your trouble," Quartermain pointed out. "Harlow can't run. A man talks big, makes a brag, then finds that he can't back out because of his pride."

"Is that what makes you walk River Street every night?"

"Maybe. I haven't figured it out yet."

Enright sighed and stood up, moving toward the front door. "Thanks for the beer," he said, and stepped out into the sunlight. Pausing there, he asked, "You going over to Doc Holderman's for supper?"

"I've been asked," Quartermain said and smiled.

The judge snorted through his nose. "When are you going to quit and marry that girl?"

Quartermain's smile deepened, wrinkling the flesh around his eyes. "That, she hasn't asked me yet."

"There's no hope for you," Enright said, and walked to his horse by the well.

After the judge left, Quartermain went back into the house and took the beer glasses to the kitchen sink where he washed them and left them upended on the drainboard. At two o'clock he mounted and rode slowly back to town.

Moving along River Street at a walk, Quartermain pulled up in front of Mammy Krieger's Saloon and dismounted. A swamper worked a broom across the wide porch, shoving the litter of a fast night ahead of him in rank clouds. He paused in his sweeping to let Quartermain pass.

Inside, the main room was cool and dim. The professor was at the piano, his nimble fingers running over a new tune. He reached for the beer sitting on the top and drank

15

deeply without dropping a beat. Behind the bar, Gil Purvis slid change and bank notes into a large canvas bag, drawing the strings tight around the puckered end. He glanced up as Quartermain came up to the bar. Purvis tossed the sack into the safe and kicked the door shut.

Reaching beneath the bar for a private bottle, he poured Quartermain a drink. He set the bottle aside and placed his hands wide along the edge of the bar, studying the marshal as he tipped up the glass. Sunlight streamed in through the wide front window, bounced against the back-bar mirror and again reflected in the polished crescent of metal pinned to Jim Quartermain's shirt.

"Tonight's the big night," Gil Purvis said. "You get any sleep?"

"An hour or so," Quartermain admitted.

"You're a fool," Purvis said. "You don't know when to quit, do you? You're twenty-seven, and in your business that's old. Lee wasn't that old when he got it and he was one of the best."

Quartermain smiled and regarded Purvis through half-squinted eyes. Unsmiling, Quartermain's face was some-what moon-shaped and bland. His eyes were large and unreadable, until he smiled. Then the lids drew together and bright splinters of light shot from the narrow gap and it changed his whole face. He wore his sideburns almost to the jaw hinge and his mustache was full and drooping to the outer edges of his lips. Quartermain raised a forefinger, brushed the mustache, then said, "You worry too much, Gil. It causes wrinkles and removes the provoca-tive bloom from your cheeks."

"Agh! Jim, did you ever think of going back to Texas?"

Quartermain once again became serious. "Yes. Many times."

"I miss it," Purvis admitted. "Why don't we both go back, Jim? I mean it. Cauldwell's offered me a good price for this deadfall and the camp's on the die-up any-way." He studied Quartermain carefully, then added, "I don't mean we have to go back to the San Saba. There's lots of room in Texas."

Quartermain searched Purvis' face and found his friend dead serious. He shook his head. "If I went back, Gil, it would be to the home place, but that belongs to Andy and Jane, not me. I never did belong there, you know that." He

16

moved his glass in an aimless circle. "After I met Lee and Bickerstaff, too many things changed. I caused the old man enough trouble when I plugged Abe Jenner."

He brightened, then, and motioned for Purvis to get himself a glass. After the drinks were poured, Quartermain raised his glass in salute. To Lee, of Texas. The Prince of the Pistoleers."

"Dead prince," Purvis amended and upped his glass. He pushed it aside and added, "Lee was no god, Jim. Neither was Bickerstaff. They were just men with magic in their hands. The same kind of magic you got."

"But Lee put it there," Quartermain said. "For better or worse, he taught me, Gil."

"A man with only one name," Purvis said. "No home, no family. Just a lost man, Jim. Did he teach you that too?"

"Why blame him?" Quartermain asked. "I don't."

"He fixed it so you'll get it like he did—in an alley and in the back." He slapped the bar and looked disgusted. "Jim, I was there. I watched it grow in you and Joel McKitrich until you weren't people any more, just men who could pull a gun and shoot. I knew Lee better than you did, Jim, and toward the last he wasn't happy. He lived in a shadow world where nothing was real to him. You're going to live there too because he willed that to you along with the skill."

Quartermain sighed and toyed with his empty whiskey glass. His voice was gentle when he said, "Let me up, Gil. I'm bleeding."

"I'm your friend," Purvis said. "You know that, Jim. Let's get out of here and go back home. Forget about Abe Jenner and think of the old man. Izee wasn't happy when you ran off. He didn't want you to go with Lee."

"I know," Quartermain said, "but it was for the best. Andy's his son and when Izee cut me in for a share of the place that wasn't right. A man passes what he has on to his blood kin, not someone he's raised just because he has a big heart."

"I know you as well as you'll let a man know you," Purvis said, "but I hate to see a man keep reachin' like you do, Jim. Maybe you'll find what you want, but I don't know."

"What do I want?" Once again Quartermain face was round and smooth and unreadable.

17

"Security. You had it once with Izee and Andy and Jane, but you gave it up to ride with Lee. Now you haven't got it and it pesters you. You keep reachin' for the little things. When a man does that, his life ain't secure and he knows it."

"Little things?"

Purvis' shoulders stirred remotely. "Like gettin' up at the same time every morning, eatin' the same thing. Like buildin' up the place out of town, then never livin' there."

For a heartbeat Quartermain studied Purvis. "I go there every day."

"Sure, to look, to fool yourself." He reached across the bar to touch his friend. "Let's go back home, Jim."

"Too late," Quartermain said, and went out to the street. He took a quick look up and down, then led his horse toward Border Street. He retied the horse in front of the doctor's large house set among the cottonwoods and ducked under the hitchrack.

The front gate squealed beneath his hand as he pushed it open and he saw Carrie Holderman come to the porch and wait. She held the screen door open for him, kissing him quickly before ushering him into the parlor. Doctor Holderman put down the paper he had been reading, rose and shook Jim Quartermain's hand. Carrie smiled and went back into the kitchen where she had an apple pie in the oven.

Doctor Ranse Holderman was a tall man and his cheeks were bearded hollows beneath high cheekbones. Hair lay thick and dark across his forehead. He waved a hand and said, "Tonight is going to be bad, Jim."

"All nights are bad on River Street," Quartermain said. "But Winn Harlow has made his last push. He's going."

"He hasn't been talking like that," Holderman said. "Some of us are getting worried, Jim. We think that once you're out of the way, Harlow will try to take Crystal City over."

"There's no doubt of it. He will."

Ranse Holderman gnawed his lip for a moment. "We've taken some measures to prevent that. Sort of a vigilante committee in case anything should happen to you. Just let Harlow try and take the town over."

"Keep that committee quiet while I'm the law," Quartermain said. "I don't like armed mobs, Ranse."

18

"This is just in case," Holderman said. "Just a spare, Jim."

Carrie rattled pots in the kitchen and Quartermain got up and went down the hall. He scraped a chair away from the table and sat down to watch her. She had on a thin cotton dress and perspiration made dark spots along the back and under her arms. It stood out in beads on her forehead and upper lip.

He said, "You shouldn't cook on a day like this. It's a hundred and five in the shade."

She brushed a strand of hair from her face. "This is what a woman does best," she said.

She was inviting him with her eyes and he stood up and put his arms around her. She came against him, raising her lips for his kiss while her arms went around his neck. Then she pulled her head back, still standing tightly against him.

"Jim, I know you love me." She turned in his arms and clasped her hands over his, holding them against the unboned softness of her waist. "Marry me, Jim. Marry me tomorrow. Tonight!"

"I couldn't do that," he said gently. "Being unsure, I couldn't."

"Let me be sure for both of us," she said. "What else matters, Jim? Don't you think I love you enough to make you happy? A woman has to make bargains, Jim. I'm willing to take a chance."

"I wouldn't let you," he said, and glanced at the wall clock. "You are a very beautiful girl, Carrie. You can make me think things I have no right to think."

"I *want* you to think them," she said fiercely. She leaned her head back against him and he kissed her lightly on the neck.

The tick of the wall clock was loud in the kitchen. He glanced at it again. "Two hours left," he said.

His reminder of the time caused her happiness to vanish. Freeing herself from his arms, she said, "I've learned to hate clocks." She stood with her back to him, her arms gripping herself tightly. "Do you think I ever sleep while you're out there? Every time a gun goes off—"

"I think your pie's burning," Jim Quartermain said.

This gave her control and the stiffness drained from her. He went down the hall, while Carrie opened the oven and craned her head aside as the blast of heat gushed forth.

Ranse Holderman had gone back to his paper so Jim Quartermain went out and sat on the front porch. Farther down the road, the Union Pacific depot sat with the drab yellow freight shed and telegrapher's shack behind it.

On his left lay the town, quiet now in the daylight hours, but at night, wild with the call of miners, hucksters, blaring with the sound of music from the half-dozen saloons. A different town when the sun died, for men came up from the creeks, pokes full of dust and a deep hunger driving them. And occasionally, a trail herd from the south would touch Crystal City for there was always a market for beef here and the cowboys would add their wildness to that of the miners.

Sitting on the porch, Quartermain saw the telegrapher leave the small building and walk toward Main Street. Then the man noticed Quartermain's horse tied by Holderman's gate and changed course. The man came on up the street, his green eyeshade pulled low over his forehead. He came through the gate and up the path, stopping by the steps. "This come for you, Marshal," he said, handing Quartermain the envelope.

Ripping it open, Jim Quartermain read the telegram twice.

JIM

ANDY DEAD. JANE AWAY. COME QUICK. WILL NOT LAST THREE MORE DAYS AT THE MOST. NEED YOU BAD, JIM.

IZEE BEAL

"Something wrong?" the telegrapher asked.

"No," Quartermain said. "No, nothing, Ewing."

The man nodded and went down the walk. Quartermain waited until the man turned toward Main Street, then went into the house. Andy dead? He remembered a tall Texan with flashing eyes and the courage of a wildcat. Dead? Where was Jane?

Not last three more days? The old man must be badly hurt. And the San Saba was a long way. Three days? Quartermain calculated it would take him three days if he took the 5:09—but he couldn't do that! There was Winn Harlow waiting at seven.

20

Frantically, Quartermain's mind raced, seeking an avenue of escape, but there was none. He had no choice, so he went back into the house and into the kitchen. He took Carrie by the arm and set her down at the table. The hands of the wall clock stood at three minutes to five. "I've got to talk to you," he said quickly and his tone brought alarm into her eyes. "Carrie, I've told you about Izee and the home place." He held up the telegram. "I've got to go back. Now. In a few minutes. I've got to catch the five-nine for Texas!"

Her eyes were wide and she didn't understand this. "But—you'll be back, won't you?" She looked past Quartermain as her father came and stood in the doorway. "Dad, Jim's going to leave!"

"I won't be able to come back to Crystal City," Quartermain said. "Carrie, understand! If I don't face Winn Harlow tonight, I'll be yellow. That's what the town will think. Can't you see that?"

"But you can show them the telegram!" She was grasping frantically. "They'll understand!"

"They won't understand," Quartermain said. "Carrie, no one will believe it and a man can't go around explaining to people."

"He's right, Carrie," Ranse Holderman said. "If he leaves, he's finished in Crystal City."

She took his arm as if to hold him. Quartermain glanced at the wall clock. Three minutes after five.

Far out on the flats a train whistle sounded long and lonesome.

"Don't go," she pleaded. "Jim, I'd rather see you fight Harlow than see you go. Please, Jim—do you have to?"

"I have to," he assured her. "Izee would never let *me* down."

"But three days—"

"I'll have a sixty mile ride when I get off the train," he said. "Carrie—" He ignored her father and pulled her to her feet, holding her tightly to him. "Carrie, there's no time now and I find there's many things I want to say to you."

She kissed him, long and hard, and her father turned away and went back to the other room. She used her lips and her body to pull at him, to hold him, but in the end she lost.

"Carrie, I'll write to you. I'll send your father a power of attorney so he can sell my place."

The train whistle was louder this time as it made a long sweep north of town. Jim Quartermain looked at her, wanting her. Then he turned and ran out the back door. She followed him to the porch as he dashed toward the depot.

"I'll follow you, Jim! Where ever you go, I'll go there too!"

Her voice faded and he ran on, pausing as he approached the depot. His wind was ragged and he pulled a twenty dollar gold piece from his pocket. "Give me a ticket to Brownwood, Texas."

The agent looked up sharply. Jim Quartermain was sweating now and streaks of it ran down his cheeks. Pulling out a ticket blank, the agent filled it in, then said, "Fourteen dollars even, Marshal."

Quartermain pocketed his change and went out on the platform to wait. The train was three miles out, the plume of smoke rising and blowing a long streamer behind the engine.

The agent came out and said, "You leaving town, Marshal?"

"That's right."

"What about Harlow?" The agent was too curious to be tactful.

Quartermain gave the man a level stare and said, "You got a gun?" The man nodded. "Then go shoot him yourself," Quartermain advised.

Nearby, the telegrapher's key rattled noisily but there was no one there to answer it. Jim Quartermain knew that the man had gone up town, spreading the word around that he was running.

He watched the train pull nearer.

No luggage, not even his gun. He counted his money. Ninety dollars. Enough for a horse and supplies at Brownwood.

The train whistled for Caslin's crossing a mile and a half out, and came on, slowing somewhat. Quartermain walked up and down the cinder platform, now and then glancing toward the head of Border Street.

He recognized Winn Harlow and Slimmie when they were still too far away to distinguish any definite feature.

Harlow was walking rapidly toward the depot with a dozen men behind him, and more gathering as he came on.

This will be a good show, Quartermain thought, immediately regretting that he did not have his gun so that he could finish the job. The thought jarred him. *You're eager to shoot a man.* Was this the sign he had been dreading? He didn't know and his worry grew larger.

The train was pulling into the depot when Harlow and Slimmie came to the building corner, stopped, then came on at a walk. Harlow was tall and handsome in a very blond way. His suit was fashionable. He wore a diamond stickpin in his Ascot tie.

And on the outside of his coat, he wore a shell belt and holstered revolver.

"Well, well," he said, smiling thinly. "Quartermain, I thought you had more guts. I really did."

Slimmie crossed his arms across his chest and grinned. He was a skinny man in faded jeans and an old cowhide vest. He kept his hands near his gun which sat on his left hip in a cross-draw holster.

"Think what you damned please," Quartermain said, and stepped onto the platform as the train stopped. Ahead, the engine puffed and exhaled steam. The brakeman and conductor went into a huddle with the agent, oblivious to any of the mounting tension on the platform.

Quartermain remained on the bottom step, one hand gripping the handrail. Harlow said, "We could have it out now."

"No gun," Quartermain said tightly.

"No gun?" Harlow laughed. "That's playing it safe, isn't it?" He swept the crowd with his eyes. "I heard about the telegram, Jim, but you really can't expect me to believe it. Seems almost too pat, don't it?"

"I thought it was timely," Quartermain said flatly. "Don't push me, Winn. I can always come back."

"You won't come back," Harlow snapped. "Run, tin-star, and keep on running. In a month, every rider passing through will know about you. The town's death to you, Quartermain. Come back and you'll get dropped before you ride a block."

The engineer applied steam and the train lurched ahead, moving slowly. Jim Quartermain remained on the bottom step and Harlow and half a hundred men paced the train to the end of the platform, jeering, laughing. When Quartermain's coach drew by, Harlow pulled his gun and shot repeatedly into the air like a cowboy hoorawing a town. Then the train was out of the station and Quartermain turned as the conductor came up.

"It's against the rules to ride on the platform, sir."

Quartermain nodded and went into the coach. He found several vacant seats and took one in the back. Within him churned a rage that was almost uncontrollable. If he had had a gun he would have jumped off and gone back to Harlow and killed him.

This knowledge that he could now hate a man so strongly was a knife in Jim Quartermain. *What's the matter with you? It's caught up with you. Now you're like Bickerstaff and Baker and the others. You're a gun dummy and all the pretty reasons won't change it.*

He forced himself to relax. He sat back in the hard seat, staring blindly at the landscape moving rearward past his window.

CHAPTER 3

When daylight began to fade and the train slowed for a town around the distant brow of a mountain, Jim Quartermain stirred and finally stood up to stretch the kinks from his back. The conductor came walking down the aisle, listing against the pull of a curve. "Canon City! Three minutes to Canon City. Change trains here for Raton, Santa Fe and El Paso."

The passengers began to gather their plunder and Jim Quartermain made his way to the vestibule, standing so that the wind didn't whip him as the train slowed for Canon City.

Damn Texas and poor railroads, he thought. A man had to go five hundred miles out of his way to get any place. The train slowed and pulled into the station. Two dozen passengers got off and stood uncertainly on the station platform. Jim Quartermain walked to the dark-

24

ened end, leaning his back against the rough siding of the depot wall. Another train sat on a spur track, making up for the southern run. He saw the conductor pacing back and forth and asked, "This the Sante Fe?"

"Southbound, yes."

Quartermain relaxed against the wall. South to home. With his eyes closed he could see the old place again, smell the hot earth and hear the movement of horses in the corral. He could see Izee Beal with his unruly mane of white hair and his booming voice and his heart full of love for horses, men and cattle. And Jane with her braids and small girl's breasts, sitting on the top bar of the corral while Andy Beal tried his temper against that of a wild horse.

That was the part of Andy he remembered, the fun loving, fighting part. Andy was like Texas, untamed, unfettered, moving where the wildness of his nature pushed him.

Quartermain found it difficult to think of Andy Beal as dead, for the boy had loved life more than anything else. Neither did he understand how Izee could be dying. The old man had never been sick a single day in his life and he seemed impervious to injury. But Izee Beal was dying, nevertheless. The old man had lived too long around animals, and like them, he would know when his final hour was approaching. Izee had never in his life asked quarter of man or beast, but now he was asking for Jim Quartermain. He must be desperate, Quartermain thought. Lonely and afraid and desperate.

That made understanding difficult, for the Beals were strong people, unafraid. Even Jane. She had her father's blood and whatever she did, she did with all her heart and energy. He smiled as he thought of her.

She would be twenty now, but he could remember her as a girl of fifteen, feeling the encroaching demands of womanhood, wanting to take life in her hands and feel it, to understand it.

The engineer pulled the whistle cord and Quartermain boarded and found himself a seat. He braced his knees against the lurch of starting, then relaxed as the train picked up speed and listened to the clack of the couplings.

At one time, he supposed, Jane Beal had loved him. She certainly claimed she did. He remembered her passion, her driving urges. She was like that in everything, wanting to taste the full measure of the nectar. Life was one glorious experiment, to be taken now, not tomorrow or when the time was ripe. Now was the only moment Jane Beal understood, the only moment she wanted to know.

He wondered if she remembered, then supposed she wouldn't. Jane forgot easily. Sensations came and went with her, and after all, they *had* been children.

Quartermain's mind swung unexpectedly to Carrie Holderman.

These two women were not alike at all, he decided. Jane would discover heretofore hidden facets of pleasure, then explore them with a certain blind recklessness. But Carrie was not like that. She studied a thing, turned it over in her mind, deciding whether she would benefit or not. Then she waited, enhancing the flavor of her emotion by drawing out her eagerness.

Quartermain sighed. Which was the answer? Would a woman's love be more real if she accepted life instantly, as she lived it? Or was it deeper and more satisfying with a woman who planned for her pleasure, building each contributing factor slowly to gather life to a pinnacle?

What are you worrying about? he asked himself. Jane Beal's not going to point a shotgun at you and force you into anything. She was little more than experimenting as a child.

But she'd be a woman now. This thought troubled Jim Quartermain.

The train rattled on and the bang of the couplings, the rattle of trucks over the rail joints, lulled him. The kerosene lamps threw a yellow glow over the interior of the coach and the door behind Quartermain opened. He heard the increased sound momentarily, then felt the breeze.

A man came down the aisle and suddenly swung into the seat facing Quartermain. Then Slimmie said, "Enjoying your ride, yellow-belly?"

His hands were casually folded across his chest, the fingertips of his right hand only inches from the butt of his gun. Quartermain took a deep breath and fastened his eyes on the man. Two seats ahead of Quartermain, three men sat in a close-packed group, talking quietly. One of

26

them looked up and saw this silent play, then nudged his two friends, bringing their attention around.

"Get the hell away from me, Slimmie," Quartermain said. "You're biting into somethin' too big to chew."

"But you got no gun," Slimmie pointed out and smiled. "I've always wanted to catch you like this." He leaned back in his seat, his eyes bold and mocking. "You rode the white horse too long, tinstar. The great big man, pushing people around—pushing me around. Now I can push you."

He raised his booted foot slowly and wiped the sole on Quartermain's dark trousers, leaving a dirty smudge. The men two seats ahead were watching carefully now, their eyes narrowed with bright splinters of interest in them.

Slimmie laughed. "You're a wind-broke horse, tinstar. I always knew the gun was what made you so damn big." He leaned forward in his seat and whipped his palm across Quartermain's face, at the same time plunging his right hand toward his gun.

The man had it all figured out before he moved. Quartermain would not take a slap in the face and Slimmie reached as he slapped, to be certain of his edge over the quiet man. But when Quartermain did not move, surprise came into Slimmie's eyes.

Slimmie's hand relaxed on the gun and he said, "What's the matt—"

Then Quartermain hit him. Jackknifing a leg, Quartermain drove the sole of his boot into Slimmie's gunhand with enough force to fracture the seat and propel him backward to the coach floor. Slimmie hit and grunted.

Quartermain came over the seat as Slimmie tried an awkward grab for his gun with his left hand. Leading with his knees, Quartermain went over the broken seat and landed on Slimmie's chest. The man shrieked in pain and heads came around and women gasped. The three men in the seats ahead laughed.

Dragging Slimmie to his feet, Quartermain hit him, an axing punch that flattened the badly injured man full length in the aisle. Bending over him, Quartermain stripped off the gunbelt and buckled it on, sliding the holster around on his right hip. Slimmie made pawing motions on the floor, trying to sit up, but he was hurt and could not make it. At the far end of the coach the conductor came through and Quartermain said, "Just leave the door open, friend."

He dragged Slimmie onto the platform between the coaches and put his foot against his rump. "You can't do that!" The conductor shouted. "He's paid his fare."

"He gets sick on trains," Quartermain said, and shoved. Slimmie went somersaulting off the train, rolling when he struck the roadbed. Quartermain went back to his seat.

As he passed the three men, one said, "You were tough on him." The man was roughly dressed. A canvas brush jacket covered his faded shirt and he wore his pistol in a shoulder holster.

"I don't make the rules," Quartermain said, and went on to the rear of the coach and sat down. He tipped his hat forward over his face and rested for several hours. He woke when the man who had spoken to him came back and sat down.

"You goin' south?" the man asked. He sized Quartermain up while he rolled a smoke. "I'm just askin'."

"The train's going that way," Quartermain said. "Does it matter to you?"

"Nothin' matters to me," the young man said, and licked his smoke. "There's money to be made in Texas, I hear. A fella in San Saba is payin' seventy a month and no work. The way you fight, I thought maybe you was going there."

"Who in San Saba?"

The man grinned behind drifting cigarette smoke. "I didn't say now, did I?" He dropped his eyes to the gun Quartermain wore, the one he had taken off Slimme. "Noticed you lifted that. You lose yours?"

Quartermain leaned forward in the seat and said softly, "Mister, why don't you go back to your friends and keep your nose out of my business before you get it out of joint."

The man's grin faded slightly and he hunched himself around in the seat, freeing his right arm. He teetered on the edge of trouble for a moment, then slapped Quartermain on the leg and said, "See you," before getting up to go back to his seat.

Quartermain leaned back and closed his eyes again. Seventy a month was gun wages. Was Izee paying that?

He decided not. The Jenners would though and the thought caused him no surprise.

The four Jenners, Kings in the San Saba. Quartermain had personally reduced the Jenners from five to four when he killed Abe. His first dead man. He recalled the deep shock after the fight. But that had soon worn off.

He thought about the Jenners: rough, womanless men who lived alone and apparently liked it. Volatile men who lived within the sphere of their narrow judgment and expected everyone else to do the same. Fists, a whip or a gun —that's what a Jenner talked with. A man either did things the Jenner way or he didn't do them at all.

That was where the trouble always lay between easygoing Izee Beal and Rob Jenner. Beal was the neighbor to the south next to the river and he leaned backward to get along with people. Rather than fight, he had let Rob Jenner have his way in the San Saba.

But Quartermain was not like Izee Beal. Not as easygoing. Lee had taught him that. He remembered how the Jenners walked soft around Lee. Walked soft and hated it. But then Lee was the greatest teacher of gunfighters who had ever lived. Not a killer, but a man who had magic in his hands and the great breath of Texas in his soul.

I guess I did Lee's killing for him, Quartermain thought. That never should have happened between me and Abe. But it *had* happened and Abe had been slow, way slow. The whole thing had been hard to explain afterward, for Abe had barely got his fingers around the butt of his gun when Quartermain's bullet caught him. He had died without clearing the holster.

Quartermain supposed that leaving Texas had been the smartest thing to do, for the split between Izee Beal's Running W and the Jenner Long Knife had widened. If I'd stuck around I'd have had to kill them all, he thought, and shifted in his seat.

He figured the traveling time up in his mind. Tonight would find him in Abilene. Probably catch a late stage out of there for Fort Griffin and Brownwood. Be daylight before he arrived. He could rent a horse, and by hard riding, raise the Running W buildings by dusk or early evening at the latest.

Crossing the flats east of El Paso, the train picked up speed and pounded along at a steady fifty-five miles an

29

hour. The land was monotonously flat and barren, with only isolated clumps of foliage to keep it from being a barren desert.

Quartermain slept through the heat of the day and with the coach windows open, coal dust and fine soot mingled with perspiration to make faces black and tempers short. That evening he checked into the Abilene station and left an hour later on the Brownwood stage. He had had time to bathe and get a shave and he felt better. Quartermain ignored the coach and climbed up on top and stretched out to sleep in the baggage rack. The metal rails would keep him from being pitched off and he gripped them with both hands, even as he dozed.

Near midnight the stage stopped for a change of horses and when the first pale streaks of dawn lightened the eastern sky, the driver dipped the four-up rig off a slight rise toward the clapboard town in the flats below.

Brownwood was three parallel streets with cross roads at each end. The driver rattled down the main street, braked to a halt in front of the hotel and threw down the mail pouch. The passengers dismounted stiffly and Quartermain was not surprised when the three men on the train got out. They stood on the boardwalk and stretched while looking the town over.

Dismounting on the other side, Quartermain walked toward the stable at the edge of town. The town was coming awake and as Quartermain walked along, he listened, noting the vast difference here, a sharp contrast to the wild voice of River Street.

He decided that the difference lay in the men, their urges, the drives that kept pushing them. This was Texas, old when the other territories were being spawned. This was his land and these were his kind of men, silent men molded by a land that tolerated no weakness. He stopped to kindle a cigar and his ears selected sounds. Men moved up the street to open their stores and he heard the soft drone of their voices. Brief words came to him, for these men did not need many. A great many of the things that men spoke of elsewhere had long been resolved here and did not need further talk.

Cattle did that to a land, he decided. Miners, timber men, trappers, all were transients, tearing up a country and then passing on. But a man could feel permanence here, in the voices, the mannerisms.

He walked on toward the stable and found the hostler asleep. Quartermain woke him and rented a close-coupled buckskin. He saddled and was leading the animal outside when the three passengers who had come in with him on the stage walked up.

The brash man in the brush jacket glanced at the saddled horse and smiled. He had wildness in his eyes and a swagger in his voice. A dangerous man, Quartermain decided. A man who measured his chances closely, then took them without a backward glance.

"I pegged you right," the man said. "You're a shooter." He shook out his makings and rolled a smoke. "I'm Audie the Kid. You probably heard of me."

"I never have," Quartermain said flatly, and saw some displeasure come into the Kid's face. That's the way with these tough ones, he thought. They pistol a man or two and expect everyone to bow because of it.

Audie the Kid jerked his thumb toward his two friends. "This is Shallak and Davis. You ever heard of them?" He laughed, a short snort in his nose. "Wait a minute until we saddle up and we'll ride with you."

"Some other time," Quartermain said.

He mounted, nudged the buckskin with his heels and rode out of town. He understood clearly what Audie the Kid and the other two were here for. And they were riding toward the San Saba. He wondered how many more would come to this town, saying little and riding out after a beer and a meal.

Men with guns and the skill to use them.

CHAPTER 4

Keeping the buckskin at a lope to save her, Jim Quartermain paused at noon, loosened the cinch and unbitted for grazing, then lay down in the sweet grass. After the buckskin cooled a bit, he mounted and pushed on.

31

He forded the Colorado at the fork near an old Comanche crossing and emerged dripping on the opposite bank. The summer's sun was a furnace. It dried him quickly, but he did not stop again until three o'clock.

Hunger clamped on his stomach but with many miles left to travel, he fought down the inclination to stop. When the buckskin showed marked signs of wear, Quartermain dismounted and walked twenty minutes, then mounted again.

The sun died slowly. The heat fell off, but the slanting rays still seared him. Soon, long shadows began to grow and he unrolled his coat and put it on. He crossed another small river, and later, a creek. The land was now so familiar that he knew exactly which way the dips and swells ran.

A man might live forever, he decided, and yet never really acquaint himself with much save the ground he called home. A man had to be a boy and chase a rabbit over a swale before he learned their runs. A boy learned where the thickets were and where the fattest grouse nested, the pastures where the grass grew sweet and where cool clear water erupted from some half hidden fissure. These things made a land home and Jim Quartermain liked the feel of it.

He was a Texan returning to his Texas.

Several miles ahead across the flats, lights made points like distant stars, flickering in the clearness of the coming night. Suddenly the trot became too plodding a pace for Jim Quartermain and he urged the buckskin into a weary run, not stopping until he flung off by the porch and went into the house with long strides.

In the front doorway he stopped. A man stood up quickly in the parlor, his hand sweeping toward the gun at his hip. Then the hand fell away and a look of incredulity came into the man's face. Hurriedly he came through the archway and into the hall.

"Jim! Jim, I'm glad you come!"

Cherokee Nye was sixty or better and his mustache hung like horse tails nearly to his chin, bobbing when he talked or moved his head. Then another man in the room stood up. He offered his hand to Jim Quartermain as he stepped into the parlor.

"Hello, Doc," Quartermain said. "How's the old man?"

"You'd better go to him," Doc Oldmeyer said.

"Sure." Quartermain turned, walking down the hall. He opened Izee Beal's door quietly, without knocking. Light from the lamp on the bed table flooded the old man's drawn face.

Izee Beal turned his head slightly and a small smile wrinkled his cheeks. Jim Quartermain threw his hat in the corner and pulled a chair close to Izee's bedside.

"Knew you'd come," Izee said. "You'd never let me down, Jim." Quartermain took the old man's hand and felt an answering pressure. "I'm not kickin'," Izee went on. "Nothin' to kick about. You'n Andy been real mavericks, but I always had a weakness for mavericks."

"Don't talk so much," Quartermain said. "We'll have lots of time to talk later."

Izee shook his head. "Been holdin' on, just waitin' for you, Jim. I'll tell you now or never tell you." He sighed and made a smoothing motion on the covers. "Andy's dead, Jim. Bushrod Jenner killed him. Parker and Forney got me."

"Why?"

Izee smiled. "Damn fool dreams I had, Jim. Wanted somethin' better than longhorns. Herefords, Jim, that's what I wanted. Saw 'em and wanted 'em." He shook his head again. "Rob Jenner objected. Blooded stock mean fences, bobwire fences. There was some arguin' and you know you can't argue with a Jenner."

He paused to cough, and after the fit passed he went on. "Andy got mad—you know how hot headed he was. Pulled on Bushrod but Bushrod beat him. Took me somewhat by surprise, and the next thing I knowed was Cherokee and some of th' boys bendin' over me."

"You hit bad?"

"Side and chest," Izee said, and blew out a weak breath. His hand came up and touched Jim Quatermain. "Jane's comin' home, boy. Cherokee wired her. You and her—well, save this for her, Jim. Do it for me. The Jenners will take this place from her unless you stop 'em." A sadness came into his eyes then. "We had ourselves a hassle, didn't we, Jim? I didn't want you to leave that time and cut you off in my will. I been sorry, boy and I changed it back long ago."

Sweat appeared on Izee Beal's face and his breathing was

ragged. Jim Quartermain stood up and looked down at this man he called 'father.' He said, "Izee, I'll be on Running W when all the Jenners are dead."

Izee Beal heard this, for he smiled. But he did not speak. Jim Quartermain went out and down the hall. The doctor and Cherokee Nye looked at him when he stopped in the archway.

"Better go to him, Doc. He's plumb tuckered." Oldmeyer nodded and hurried away, while Quartermain lighted a cigar from the lamp chimney. The cook came in with a tray of sandwiches and a pint of beer and Quartermain put down his cigar to eat.

"You stayin'?" Cherokee asked.

"Yes."

"Then he'll die happy." The old Texan rolled a cigarette and struck a match on his boot sole. "McKitrich came back, Jim."

"Joel?" Quartermain paused with the beer half-raised to his lips.

"Three years ago," Cherokee said. "You know what's goin' on around here?"

"No." Quartermain put a match to his cigar. He walked over to the fireplace and leaned his arms against the mantle, standing with his back to Cherokee Nye.

"Izee sold off every damn head he owned. The boys built a small fence south of the barn and we're holdin' a hundred head of Herefords."

"So?"

"So Rob Jenner don't like it. He claims the range is goin' to stay open and we're goin' to raise longhorns like we always done. I heard a rumor that he'd back his talk with lead."

"You think he wants war?"

Cherokee snorted. "Hell, no! He wants his own way. There's some changes goin' on in Texas, Jim. This is eighteen eighty and things is different. Lot of little fellas startin' up and a man's got to think ahead. 'Nother ten years and a man'll be big if he owns nine thousand acres instead of fifty thousand. Personally, I like Herefords better. The beef's better. You don't have to raise so many and a man can work a smaller crew 'cause they ain't so damn wild. Fencin' seems to be the only rub."

34

Quartermain turned to look at Cherokee. "The Jenners know I'm here?"

Cherokee shook his head. "Just me and Cimarron. I guess McKitrich knows. He was over here yesterday askin'."

"How many men on the payroll?"

"Nine."

"Not enough."

"It was enough," Cherokee said. "Take this right, Jim, but when you and Lee rode out that day we thought we'd seen the last of you. This could shape up to a big fight. Maybe you wouldn't want it."

"I told Izee I'd stay," Quartermain said.

"He won't last until morning," Cherokee opined. "After that, who's to know what you do?"

"I'd know," Quartermain said, "and you'd know."

"I don't count," the old man said. "You doing this for Jane?" When Quartermain looked sharply at him, Cherokee seemed momentarily uncomfortable. He walked to the fireplace and threw his cigarette away. "Well, you and her was pretty close."

"She'll be a woman now," Quartermain said, "and she's liable to feel a lot different than when she left here. If I was you, I wouldn't embarrass her with something she's probably eager to forget."

"Sure," Cherokee said. He walked to the hallway. "You're to sleep in the house, Jim. Izee wants it that way now."

"All right," Quartermain said, and listened to the old man thump down the hall and off the front porch.

He considered his position here and felt out of place. Once he had torn up his roots, expecting the plant to die, but he found that it had not. The familiarity of the old place, the feel of the floor creaking beneath his feet, washed out the years he had been away.

But I don't want a shooting war, he told himself. He gnawed on the end of his cigar and drew acrid smoke into his lungs. He knew what range warfare was like—a bloody, undisciplined fight with the right and wrong so mixed up that no man could untangle it.

Jim Quartermain wanted no part of it. Being a marshal had been bad enough, even with the law-and-order factions stoutly behind him. Justice somehow always removed

35

the taint from a killing. But here a man had only his judgment to back him and this could cause a lot of strain.

Doctor Oldmeyer came into the room and crossed to the fireplace. He discarded a bloody cloth and a wadded handful of bandages. Glancing at Quartermain, he sighed and said, "Not more than an hour or two."

Oldmeyer was a heavy man and his face was lined with the troubles of many people. His hands were huge and hairy and very gentle. He accepted one of Quartermain's cigars, along with a match, and after he got it puffing properly he said, "I don't know where he gets the heart. He should have died last night or the day before yesterday. There's not enough blood left in him to fill a chicken."

"How did Andy get it?"

"Clean," Oldmeyer said. "Through the neck. He must have bled out in a matter of minutes." He studied the growing ash on his smoke, then added, "When Andy's horse came back, Cherokee went out."

"The Jenners left Izee for dead then?"

Oldmeyer nodded. "I went over to Rob Jenner's place yesterday afternoon. They didn't deny it. Andy drew first and Izee had to back his hand."

"He was the kind," Quartermain said. "Andy's hot head once in a while got him into trouble." He lifted his eyes to Oldmeyer. "Cherokee said Joel McKitrich is back."

"Yes. He's ranching a place ten miles south of here." Oldmeyer's brows wrinkled and he gnawed on his cigar. "Joel's quit, Jim. Out and out quit. He's married and got a year old boy."

"He said he'd quit," Quartermain said, "but I didn't believe it. People won't let you once you get known." He glanced at Oldmeyer. "Which side is he on, Doc?"

"No side," Oldmeyer stated. "McKitrich is on the fence and he's going to stay that way. Andy tried to get him with Running W, but Joel wouldn't come in. Rob Jenner didn't have any better luck."

"Jenner could use a gun like McKitrich," Quartermain said. "I saw him in action in Dodge City nearly four years ago. He's hard to beat."

"Rob hasn't hired any guns," Oldmeyer said. "He's been goin' around bellerin' like a nutted bull, but then, he always does when something don't suit him. You going to take up the stick for Izee, Jim?"

"I'm staying, if that's what you mean. You think I shouldn't?"

The doctor's shoulders rose and fell. "Other than pills, I give people little advice. But the smart thing for you to do would be to ride out. Staying would just be waving a red flag under Rob Jenner's nose. They hated Bob Lee because he never bowed to them. A man as fast as he was didn't have to. You and Lee were close, Jim, so what they felt toward him was passed on to you. Then you shot Abe." He sighed and knocked ashes off his smoke. "It isn't the fight over the fences that worries me, Jim. It's what this does to you inside."

"What's it doing?" Quartermain asked.

Oldmeyer settled himself in a chair with a tired grunt and crossed his legs. He drew on his cigar until he coughed, then said, "I knew Hickok before his Abilene days, Jim, and I watched him change. Sitting in corners or against the wall all the time. I heard that he wrinkled paper and put it on the floor at night so that he would have a second's warning in case anyone tried to get to him. Living on the thin edge eats at a man, Jim, and finally he can't walk past a dark alley or stand in front of a window. It's happened to the best of them, believe me."

"What's a man supposed to do?" Quartermain asked softly.

"Quit. Just up and quit. Then when some tough comes up, take his sass and forget about it." He slapped his legs and stood up. "Why worry about it now? You've got enough to think about. Jim, remember that the Jenners don't want to fight either. They just don't want any fences. If you pulled out, Running W would back down and that'd be the end of it."

"And if I stay?"

"They'll fight until you're burned to the ground."

"Sure," Quartermain said. "That's the way it'll be. The Jenners win if I leave or stay, is that it?"

"You always claimed to face the facts," Oldmeyer said, "so face this one."

"Not easy," Quartermain admitted. "You know where Jane is?"

37

"St. Louis school for girls. She'll be different, Jim. The rough edges will be gone."

"You don't knock the rough edges off a Beal that easy," Jim Quartermain said. He tossed his sour cigar into the fireplace and Oldmeyer gathered his hat and black bag.

"I'll bunk with Cherokee tonight," he said. "I suppose you'll be with him?"

"Yes," Quartermain said, and watched the doctor go out.

He entered the old man's room quietly and found Izee Beal awake. The lamp was still bright by the bedside and Jim Quartermain pulled his chair close.

"It's nice this way, Jim."

"Try and get some rest, Izee."

"Rest? I'm headin' for a long one." His hand moved aimlessly over the covers, so white and thin that Quartermain could count the veins. He could not associate these hands with Izee Beal. Not the Izee Beal who had built an empire with rope and gun.

"Got no regrets," Izee said. "Not a one." He studied Jim Quartermain with eyes that were bright and probing even on the verge of death. "You ain't changed much. A little more serious, maybe, but you always was a serious one. Wanted to know this and that. You ever figure out all them answers, son?"

"Some of them," Quartermain admitted. "Some I didn't like."

"It goes that way," Izee murmured. "Lee used to worry me some, the influence he had on you. But I guess it worked out for the best. You won't like what I've laid out for you, Jim, but I had to do it."

"It's all right, Izee."

"Yeah, you'd say that." He rolled his head slowly toward the lamp and added, "You mind turnin' that up? Likely needs kerosene."

Jim Quartermain straightened in his chair, then spoke gently. "The lamp's all right, Izee."

"Huh?" Then awareness came to the old man and he relaxed. He lay with his eyes wide open, breathing evenly, his lined face composed and without fear.

"Always wondered what it'd be like," he said. "Nothin' to fear. Somethin' every man's got to face." Moving his head a little, he focused his eyes on Jim Quartermain.

38

"Can't hardly see you now, but I know you're there. Real comfortin', Jim, knowin' you're there."

He tried to smile, but the muscles did not quite make it. His breath left him in a long sigh and then he relaxed completely. For a minute Jim Quartermain sat motionless. Then he pulled the sheet over Izee Beal's face.

Turning the lamp down until the room was deeply shadowed, he sat there for the better part of an hour, rousing himself only when he heard the front door open and close. He stepped into the hall and Cherokee Nye stopped. Quartermain shook his head once, then walked on past Nye and into the parlor.

CHAPTER 5

Izee Beal was buried in the shade of the cottonwood grove west of the house. By noon, families began to gather. At one, the undertaker came back from town, a cadaverous man with a flapping coat who alternated his time between cutting hair and preaching when the occasion demanded.

Jim Quartermain stood on the inner edge of the circle near the new grave, turning away and walking back to the house when the crowd dispersed. The people assembled in his parlor, not saying much, just drinking the coffee and eating the sandwiches the cook had prepared. Quartermain did not know any of these people and they exhibited no inclination to get acquainted.

They were poor and they wore wash-faded clothes. The marks of hard work were upon all of them. Quartermain let his eyes rove around the room until he saw Cherokee Nye standing in the corner, talking to a tall, raw-boned man.

Quartermain pushed his way through the crowd and took the man's arm.

"Joel McKitrich!"

McKitrich smiled as he extended his hand. He spoke in a soft, deep bass. "You look the same, Jim, which is a surprise. Glad to see it though."

Cherokee leaned his back against the living room wall and watched these people while he fashioned a cigarette. "The country's fillin' up with these squatters," he said significantly. "Th' word's goin' around that you're on the throne, Jim. They're curious as to what you're going to do about 'em."

Quartermain studied the guests, then spoke to Joel McKitrich. "Your wife among them?"

McKitrich nodded. "You won't be able to tell her from the others, Jim. They're all alike, poor, and worried now. Izee tolerated 'em, but Izee's dead. You may not want 'em and they're waitin' to see."

"They squat along the river bottom," Cherokee said, putting a match to his smoke. "Rob Jenner runs 'em off with a rifle. Be smart if you'd do th' same."

"You and Izee didn't see eye to eye then, it seems."

"Sometimes we didn't. A man's a fool to give up land he's fought for. These squatters don't care. They've been pushed around before."

"I see," Quartermain said. He remained thoughtfully silent for a moment, then said, "Hitch up the buggy and drive to Brownwood. Jane will probably come in on to-night's stage. Wait for her until she does come."

"Now?" Cherokee's face filled with annoyance.

"There's no better time," Quartermain said, and watched him stomp angrily out of the house. Through the window, Quartermain could see him crossing the yard. Then he turned his attention back to Joel McKitrich.

McKitrich was a man in his middle thirties, a quiet man with dark eyes and a grave manner that went with hard work and too little fun. His hands were slender, the fingers lumpy along the knuckles. He wore his hair long and a close clipped mustache filled his upper lip. He said, "You shouldn't get sore, Jim. Cherokee'll never change."

The talk died off and these people stood motionless, watching Jim Quartermain. He said, "I don't know any of you, except McKitrich here. But Izee Beal left the future of Running W in my hands and any policy he had with honest men I will honor to the end. Should you find yourself pressed, Running W is always good for a side of beef or a sack of flour. But if I find a hide on any man's place and he hasn't asked, he'll leave." He paused and swept them with his eyes. "I thank you for coming to the old man's funeral. Izee Beal was a man who liked his friends around him."

Quartermain walked out, leaving them behind to talk this over. Joel McKitrich followed him to the edge of the porch and rolled a smoke. By the barn, Cherokee was hitching a matched pair of bays to an open buggy. Both men watched as he drove from the yard, the wheels whipping up dust like thick wood smoke.

McKitrich wiped a match against the porch post. "You meant that in there, Jim?"

"Did I do wrong?"

"No," McKitrich said. "They'll treat you right." He smiled then and his teeth were white and even. "Should you make Rob Jenner behave and raise Herefords, you'll need these squatters. They raise hay and feed, Jim—pretty precious items to a man who hand feeds during the winters."

"Where do you stand in this, Joel?"

"Between you and Jenner?" He laughed. "Nowhere, Jim. I've got out of the business. I sleep good nights. No more dark streets and crazy kids with guns after a reputation."

"Then you're lucky," Quartermain said, and left the porch. He walked to the corral where Cimarron watched two men saddle an unbroken stud. Cimarron was a man in his early thirties, tall and slow talking. He wore his mustache handlebar fashion and his eyes, when they swung to Quartermain were a startling shade of blue. He was a handsome man in a half-ferocious way, for he possessed a nervousness that made him high-strung.

"Saddle two horses," Quartermain said. "We're going to town."

He did not wait for an answer, but crossed again to the house for Slimmie's gun and holster. He came out a few minutes later, buckling this on. Cimarron came up with the horses and they mounted. They rode out at a walk, and for a mile, neither man spoke. But finally Jim Quartermain said, "Izee buy the fencing yet?"

Cimarron nodded. "It's in the warehouse at McKeogh and Shipley's Store."

"We'll take it back with us then," Quartermain said matter-of-factly.

Cimarron shot Quartermain a glance that was warm with interest. "Rob Jenner says 'No.'"

"And I say we'll take it with us tonight. The post holes dug?"

"Dug and the poles set." Cimarron said. "You really goin' to string wire?"

"That's what it's for." Quartermain nipped the end off a cigar with his teeth. He scratched a match on the saddle-horn and cupped his hands around it. Dropping his glance to Cimarron's waist, he saw the gutta-percha handled Colt there. "You still think you're pretty good with that?"

Cimarron grinned. "As good as most."

"I may need a man who's better than most," Quartermain said.

The shine in Cimarron's eyes was brighter now. "I've heard you're better than Lee ever was. That's quite a reputation to have."

"You may get your chance to earn one," Quartermain said, and drew deeply on his cigar.

The heat was heavy and he removed his coat, draping it across his knees. The horses' hooves plopped in the dust and raised small bombs in thin clouds. "You ever been to Rob Jenner's place since the shooting?"

Cimarron's manner became cautious. "Once or twice. Why?"

"Go there now. Tell him I'm in town and want to talk. Remember, talk—not fight."

"Hell," Cimarron said, "I ain't friendly with that tribe. They're liable to start shootin' was I to show up there."

"Leave your gun with me," Quartermain said. "A Jenner would as soon shoot himself as he would an unarmed man." He waited while Cimarron seesawed back and forth. Finally the lanky man unbuckled his shell belt and handed it over. "I'll leave this hanging on the saddlehorn," Quartermain said, and watched Cimarron veer off to the right and meet the road a mile beyond.

Ahead, Cherokee's buggy raised a plume of dust, but Quartermain did not try to catch up with him. The town lay an hour's ride away and he held the buckskin to a walk. He saw the dark outline ahead and watched it grow larger until he reached the end of the main street.

The one street was flanked by a double row of false fronts. A hotel stood on the near corner, across from the saloon. The stable was at the far end, beyond a string of smaller business houses.

Dismounting by the hotel, Quartermain tied his horse and walked down the street to the little bank. The room was cool and dim, hidden from the sun's blast, and he found Horace Pendergast in his small office. Pendergast got up, shook Quartermain's hand and said, "Jim, by golly now! Come on in."

He saw Quartermain seated and that he had a fresh cigar, then sat down behind his desk with his fingertips placed evenly together. "I was wondering if you'd come back, Jim. The country is headed for the skids and we need a man like you to take a grip on things."

"What kind of a man am I, Horace?"

The banker floundered for a moment. "Well, your reputation is pretty big, Jim. You know what I mean." He laughed and leaned forward, his smile genuine. "Are you going to buck Rob Jenner?"

Quartermain sighed and toyed with his cigar. "Buck him? Yes. Fight him? Not if I can avoid it." He shifted in the hard-backed chair and crossed his legs. "Fighting won't build, Horace. As a banker you know what a good quarrel can do to a country. A man is drawn into it whether he wants to come or not."

"Big things come out of wars," Pendergast said. "I have a theory about wars. I believe that only a culturally superior, mentally superior race can subjugate another plan or people. Of course, there's suffering for awhile, but eventually the conquered benefit from war in increased learning, culture, and so forth. Interesting?"

"But impractical in Texas," Quartermain said. "There are a lot of new people around here, Horace. Little people who are just getting started. A fight will put them in the middle."

"It puts *me* in the middle," Pendergast said, and rose to go to his filing cabinet. He withdrew several sheets of paper and tossed them on the desk. "These are mortgages, Jim. Taken in faith and now not worth the paper they're written on." He slapped his palm with them. "These people came to me broke. Broke but honest. They needed money to work the land until they could prove up on it and I gave them money. There was no hint of trouble then and everything looked fine. Now it looks very bad."

"You sound like a big-hearted man," Quartermain said.

Pendergast sighed. "Would you let them starve? Or steal and get hung for it?"

"Considering that it was Running W and Long Knife money you were loaning, I can't say that I blame you for being generous."

Pendergast flushed. "I don't deserve that, Jim! I'm the founder of this bank and the major stockholder. If anyone's going to lose, it'll be me."

"That may be," Quartermain said. He pursed his lips and turned a new thought over in his mind before speaking of it. "Between you and me, Horace, how many of these squatters have proved up on the land?"

Pendergast's lips pulled down, then relaxed. "Seventy per cent. But that don't pay off these mortgages. Something on your mind, Jim?"

"I was just thinking that a man is more inclined to fight if he's got somethin' to lose."

"Ah! So it *is* fight?"

"You know the Jenners. You figure it, Horace."

"I already have," Pendergast said, and watched Jim Quartermain walk out. He waited until he could no longer see Quartermain, then signaled for the young bookkeeper. "Go over to the saloon and tell Audie the Kid to come here. Tell him to use the alley door."

When the young man hurried out, Horace Pendergast sat hunched over in his chair, his fingers drumming the sheaf of mortgages on his desk.

And in the mercantile, Quartermain found Vrain McKeogh in the back room checking his inventory. Quartermain paused in the doorway and said, "I hear you got a shed full of wire for Running W."

McKeogh straightened, a wiry little man with red hair. "I have. Also got a bet that Running W will never get it out of town."

"Whose side are you on?"

"No side," McKeogh said. "Logic, that's what I use. Built my business on logic, not sentiment. The Jenners say you're not goin' to take the wire out. Been here a month now and Izee Beal couldn't swing it. Tried twice. The last time men got killed arguin' over it."

"They say the third time's a charm," Quartermain said,

and went through the store and back to the street. At the livery stable he rented two high-sided wagons and drove them to the rear of McKeogh and Shipley's store, parking them by the loading platform. McKeogh came out and said, "You're a smart one, Jim. All sentiment and no logic. Was you logical you wouldn't even be in this part of Texas."

"*You* be logical," Quartermain said, and jumped down. "See that these wagons are loaded by seven o'clock."

"I'll attend your funeral," McKeogh said. He yelled for a half grown boy to get busy, watched Quartermain go through the store and said, half to himself, "Such a nice young fella too."

Quartermain ate at the hotel, his first good meal of the day. The wall clock stood at five and he dawdled over his second cup of coffee. A rider came into town and swung off across the street. Cimarron went into the saloon and came right out. He saw Quartermain's horse then and came across the street, pausing only long enough to remove his gunbelt from the saddle-horn and buckle it on.

"They'll be here before dark," he said as he came in and sat down. His shirt was dusty and damp with sweat. He shook out the makings and spun a smoke. "There's too many, Jim. You better wait until you get some men behind you."

"I don't need men to talk," Quartermain said. "Clean up and eat."

"Sure," Cimarron said, and went into the back room to wash.

Exactly at six, Jim Quartermain returned to the mercantile to check his wagons. He found them loaded and parked in the alley. He retraced his steps back to the hotel. The sun was dying, and with it, the shocking heat. Long shadows formed in the streets between the buildings and he took a seat on the hotel porch.

Cimarron exited from the saloon across the street, wiping his mouth with his sleeve. He stood along the wall, a tall, loose-muscled man with a latent danger on his face. Watching him, Quartermain decided that he knew a good deal about the Cimarrons who moved around the West. They were rash men, neither expert nor completely inefficient with their weapons, and in a country where proficiency counted they found themselves at odds both ways to the ace.

He had met his share of these men, all eager to fight and gain a reputation that would elevate them. Quartermain decided that he had been lucky, for he had wounded three and talked the other odd dozen out of any rash act.

Out on the flats, a party of horsemen drummed nearer. From the other direction, a stage topped the brief rise northwest of town and tipped down to follow the curving road.

Quartermain focused fully on the approaching riders. He had lived in this country most of his life and he knew that sound, the drumming pound of the Jenners riding.

They were nearer now. Near enough to distinguish one from the other. Rob Jenner's flowing dark beard. The hulking shoulders of Bushrod. Parker, the slim one, almost like a woman with his graceful manners. Forney, slow-witted and dangerous as a bear when aroused.

The sound of the approaching stage was a rattle that built steadily in volume as it drew closer. The clatter of chains and the squeak of a dry axle came clearly across the remaining distance.

They entered the town together, the Jenners and the stage from Fort Chadbourne. The stage pulled up in front of the hotel with smoking brake blocks and stopped in a swirling cloud of thick dust. This was the hour of yellow sky, of deepening dusk, and Jim Quartermain stood up, throwing his cigar into the street.

Across from him, the Jenners sat their mounts, their eyes fastened on Quartermain. His attention was fully on them when the stage door opened and Carrie Holderman said, "Jim!"

CHAPTER 6

Jim Quartermain came numbly down the steps, took Carrie's arm and helped her from the stage.

"What are *you* doing here?" he asked.

46

The stage swayed as Gil Purvis got down, stamping his feet to restore circulation in his legs. He wore a new suit and a flowing tie tucked into an embroidered vest.

He said, "Surprised?"

Quartermain sighed with some exasperation and looked at Carrie. She studied his face in the half light, a grave girl, uncertain now of his disposition. "I told you I'd follow you, Jim. Didn't you believe me?"

"Yes," he said. "Yes, Carrie. I believed you."

Purvis shifted his feet slightly and said, "We goin' to stand here all night? Hell, I brought her, so let's see that Texas hospitality."

Quartermain guided her up the hotel steps and into the lobby. Across the street, saddle leather creaked as the Jenners dismounted. Gil Purvis murmured, "Oh, oh. Ol' ugly's still around."

Pausing before the desk, Jim Quartermain said, "The lady would like a room, please."

He laid a twenty dollar gold piece on the desk blotter. The clerk extended a key and Jim Quartermain took it as boots rattled across the porch and the Jenners came into the room to pause just inside the door.

Rob Jenner thrust his huge head forward like an animal keening the wind. His sons were arrayed behind him in a loose string. Parker, the thin one, pushed by his brother, Forney. Parker was big enough to wear guns now and they sat in cross-draw holsters on each hip. The pearl handles picked up the lamplight and cast it back, multicolored and sparkling

Then Rob Jenner moved deeper into the room, his sons following, their Mexican rowel spurs clanking across the bare floor like loose chains. They brought with them the smell of danger, of inflexible will and cruel power.

Taking Carrie Holderman's arm, Quartermain walked toward the stairs. Gil Purvis sagged against a column and said, "Guess I'll stay and keep Mr. Jenner and his boys company. Care for a drink, gents?"

The old man's head turned stiffly. He stared at Purvis. Here was a man who had worn the Running W brand for years, an old enemy of the Jenners, but a Texas man nevertheless. The drink had been offered in friendliness and frontier protocol dictated that the Jenners should drink, forgetting the past for the moment.

"My pleasure," Rob Jenner said, and motioned for his boys to belly up to the small hotel bar.

Quartermain went to the second floor with Carrie and unlocked her door for her. He went in ahead of her and lighted two lamps while a boy trudged up the stairs with her baggage. Quartermain motioned toward the corner. The boy set them down and went out, closing the door behind him.

Carrie stripped off her gloves and took off her hat, laying these things on the bed. She brushed at the dust covering her dark dress. It filmed her hair and lay like powder on her face.

"I don't think you're glad I came," she said.

He had intended to remain somewhat detached, even distant, but he could not resist the soft pull of her voice.

"Carrie," he said, and took a step toward her.

She came to him frankly, honestly, her lips searching for his. He kissed her with a longing he had not wished to reveal and at last she leaned back, still in his arms. "You *are* glad."

"This is not too wise," he said. "This isn't your parlor."

The lighting of a cigar gave function to his hands. She watched his face and eyes, smiling, for she knew how much he needed her and how hard he was trying to cover that need.

"Is your father coming?"

"No, Jim. I came with Gil Purvis."

He frowned. "Proper ladies don't think of things like this, let alone do them."

"A woman in love is not a proper lady," Carrie said. "Although not many want to admit it. Were you in time, Jim?"

He nodded. "He died a few hours after I got here." The cigar tasted bitter to him and he rolled it between his fingers, examining it. "I'm the boss now and Running W is half mine. I'm not sure whether I like it or not."

"Those men that came in downstairs—they're not your friends, are they."

"Those are the Jenners," he said. "I'd like it if they weren't openly enemies either." He sighed and blew out a cloud of thin smoke. "Likely I'll fight them, but they've come here tonight to talk, a thing they don't do too well."

48

"I believe I've interrupted something," she said. "Was that the reason you were displeased?"

"Carrie, I wasn't displeased." He took her arms and held her lightly. "Just overwhelmed," he said, and kissed her again. "When I go back to the ranch tonight, I'll take you with me."

Her smile teased him. "A moment ago you were worried about my coming here seeming awkward. Won't this look strange, Jim?"

"Jane Beal will be home tomorrow or the next day," he said. "It'll be all right."

A new seriousness moved into her eyes, shoving the laughter out. "Does everything always have to be perfect, Jim? Can't we play the game one time without shuffling the cards?" She turned and opened a canvas valise. "I got this from your desk," she said and handed him his .44 Remington, complete with belt and holster.

He unbuckled Slimmie's gun and tossed it on the bed. She watched him while he adjusted the harness with practiced movements of his fingers. "I didn't want to bring it," she said. "That gun is a rival of mine and I'm jealous. I never thought a thing of steel could arouse such a strong emotion in me, but it does. I'd like to drop it down a well so deep that you could never get it out."

Quartermain snapped it up from the holster and half-cocked it. "It's loaded," she said. "Six bullets."

"Carrie," he said, "wait here. I'll be back soon."

"I know." She followed him to the door and stood there until he disappeared below the top of the stairs. Then hearing a man's voice grumbling down below, she went back inside and closed the door.

Rob Jenner and his boys were lined up at the hotel bar when Jim Quartermain stopped by the small ell where Gil Purvis stood. Quartermain placed his hands flat on the polished surface, in plain sight.

"I take it we've come here to talk," he said. "All right, we might as well speak out."

"I done my talkin' to Izee Beal," Rob Jenner said, his voice like heavy thunder. "Th' only reason me'n my boys come in was to tell you to your face."

"The old man's gone," Quartermain said. "Now I'm the boss of the Running W."

"Sure he's gone, and I shot him," Parker Jenner said.

49

He stepped away from the bar, his hands hooked in his belt. "I been hearin' how good you are, Jim. You want to try your luck with me? I didn't need no Lee of Texas to teach me either."

Rob Jenner rumbled, "Park, you shut your face and get back behind me where you belong."

"There stands the man who killed Abe—"

Rob Jenner flung his huge arm back and caught Parker in the chest with the back of his hand, knocking the young man against the bar. "Hold your peace there, wild one! Abe got his fair and square, so there's no complaints now, you understand? We come here in peace and no Jenner will break it, get me."

The old man faced Quartermain. "String no wire, boy. Fence no land that a Jenner rides across."

"You ranch Long Knife," Quartermain said, "and leave Running W business to me."

"Ha!" Jenner said, and slapped the bar. "You think I'm a fool? If you fence, that forces me to fence too. I'm keepin' my money, not stringin' it out on poles."

"I want no trouble between us," Quartermain said. "I ask you now to meet Running W halfway. If we can't be friends, then we'll leave each other alone."

"I make no bargain with man or animal," Rob Jenner declared. "I've never had to and I never will. That's my flat word." He shifted his weight and leaned his elbow on the bar. "I come to this country as a boy. There was nothin' but Comanche lodges and buff'lo. Buried my woman and three daughters and a son in Texas soil. I play rough, mind you. Like it that way, so bear it mind. You fools can go ahead and dream all you want about how safe you're goin' to make the country, but I don't have to do it. Raise schools, make laws, pin a badge on some mucklehead so's he can strut around—that's not for me. I like it like I got it. Don't want nothin' different."

"You know," Quartermain said, "you've never been licked and it's gone to your head." Quartermain offered this challenge gently and watched it eat into Rob Jenner's pride. He knew the man well, understood him, for Jenner was a simple man, not stupid, but elemental in his emotions. He could love or hate with equal violence.

"Well," Jenner said dangerously, "I could give you a chance to hand me one."

50

"With fists," Quartermain said, and smiled. "You'd never match me with a gun."

"I'll match you with anything you name!" Jenner flared.

Gil Purvis shifted by Quartermain's elbow and said, "Easy now. He wasn't just flappin' his mouth, Jim. He's rough."

"Let's find out how rough," Quartermain said.

He unbuckled his gunbelt, slapping it down hard on the bar. Rob Jenner laughed and removed the pistol from beneath his coat, sliding it toward Quartermain's gun. Then he stepped away and shrugged his shoulders.

Rob Jenner was six feet tall and solidly muscled. He was near sixty, but age had not softened him in mind or body. Quartermain let him come within reach then shot away from the bar like a released spring. His fists broke through Jenner's raising guard and battered the man across the nose. Jenner bellowed and swung, but Quartermain bobbed off in the clear, waiting for the big man to advance.

This was the surprise, he told himself, the lucky punch, and he knew he would not get another. The fight would get rough now and Jenner would make Quartermain work, paying dearly to land a solid blow. Quartermain had hurt Jenner, but pain had no permanent effect on the man.

Rob Jenner charged like an enraged bull, head down, arms flailing.

Trying to duck aside, Quartermain caught one of Jenner's thrashing fists and the blow carried him backward halfway across the room. Quartermain struck the wall with a numbing force as Rob Jenner veered toward him. Sinking quickly, Quartermain let a wild blow pass over his head and then Jenner yelled as his fist struck the wall.

Jabbing with his feet, Quartermain threw the man backward, across a heavy French monte table, and onto the floor. Rolling as he came erect, Quartermain followed Jenner and was ready when the man made his feet. The man's right hand sported two broken knuckles and Jenner let the arm dangle, content to fight the rest of the way with his left.

Quartermain struck Jenner on the bridge of the nose again and once on the cheekbone, all the time weathering the punishment of Jenner's left hand. The big man staggered back a step but did not go down. He hit Jim Quartermain alongside the head and watched him skid on the sawdust covered floor. Quartermain's sliding body cut the legs from under a small table and came to rest against the wall.

Rob Jenner stood flat-footed in the middle of the floor, blood dripping from his nose. He did not move in, but waited while Quartermain pushed himself erect again. Quartermain approached Jenner cautiously and the man tried to fend him away with his left hand, all the time circling to the left. Allowing Jenner to set the pace, Quartermain waited until Jenner advanced, then broke away, slamming into Jenner.

The suddenness with which Quartermain changed pace took Jenner by surprise and Quartermain belted the man solidly along the jaw and once in the stomach before dashing out of reach. Jenner's left hand dropped and Quartermain came in from the left quarter, striking him a driving blow that left Jenner's eyes round and dull.

Jenner tried to take a step and the strength left him. His knees wilted like melting candles and then he fell limply into the sawdust and lay still. Along the bar a sudden flurry of movement drew Quartermain away from Rob Jenner.

Gil Purvis said, "Don't do it, Parker!"

Purvis had lifted Quartermain's gun and was holding the hammer back with the palm of his left hand. Parker Jenner let his revolver slide back into his holster and turned his back to the room, his elbows planted solidly on the bar.

Quartermain retrieved his gun from Purvis and put it on. His breathing was ragged and blood trickled down his left cheek. The side of his face carried a deadness from Jenner's fists. Jenner was stirring, trying to sit up. He raised his head and looked around the room.

"Did one of my sons pull his pistol?" Blood dripped off his chin and one eye was beginning to close.

"Let it go," Jim Quartermain said.

Cimarron came in then, stopping in the doorway. He looked at the Jenner boys lined along the bar, and Rob standing now, his face battered. "I missed something," he said dryly, and leaned against the wall.

"Did one of my boys flourish a weapon?" Rob Jenner repeated. "I mean to be answered, dammit!"

Purvis said, "Parker had an idea."

"So!" Rob Jenner said. He swiveled his head to his youngest son and Parker saw what was coming. Parker pushed away from the bar, trying to make the door, but his father caught him. He grabbed the boy by the collar and slammed him in the face with his fist. "So!" Rob shouted. "So my boy pulls his pistol!"

Parker tried to fight back, but Rob Jenner battered the boy's arms aside and slapped him several times across the face. "A fair fight and you flourish your pistol!" he raved. "Dadblamed varmint! I brung you up different than that."

He muscled Parker to the floor and held him scissored between his legs while he stripped the boy of his weapons. Throwing these to the other Jenners, he gave Parker a shove and straightened.

"I apologize for my boy's actions," Rob said. He glowered at Parker who lay on the floor. "Get to your feet!"

Parker's face was darkly surly, but he obeyed. He went back to the bar and leaned on it, scrubbing the back of his hand across his bleeding mouth.

Stepping away from the bar, Quartermain spoke quietly. "Gil, are you looking for work or are you too rich to think about it?"

"I'm never that rich," Purvis said. "What do I do?"

"Take Cimarron with you and pick up one of the wagons thats' parked behind McKeogh and Shipley's Store. Drive one out. Cimarron can take the horses. I'll follow you in the other."

Purvis glanced at the Jenners and moved away from the bar. Cimarron followed him out. Rob Jenner scrubbed a hand across his battered face and shook his head. "I didn't want this, Quartermain. Indeed I didn't. Don't string no wire. I'd rather you didn't now."

"People have got to change with the times," Quartermain said. "Let's not have any trouble over it. The wire's going to Running W tonight."

"I can't back down on my word," Rob Jenner said. "Man, you're making me fight you now."

"Two to one," Quartermain pointed out. "Parker's guns are on the bar. So are yours. Forney's slow, Rob. I'd get him easy. I can beat Bushrod and you know it. That's

53

two dead men, Rob, just because you can't take back something you said."

"I don't like it," Jenner said bleakly, "but you're forcin' me."

A step creaked as someone came down the stairs and the Jenners looked around. Rob Jenner was surprised and angry when Carrie Holderman crossed the small barroom and stood between them and Jim Quartermain. She presented her back squarely to the Jenners.

"Will I have to ride in the wagon, Jim?"

Her face was flushed and her fists tightly clenched. She was afraid but hiding it well. This was no stupid woman, or a weak one, Quartermain knew. She had good steel in her and she was a fighter. Carrie had walked into this, fully aware of the building danger, and she was neutralizing the Jenners as effectively as if she were covering them with a shotgun.

Quartermain smiled. "As soon as these gentlemen are through talking, we'll go." He met Rob Jenner's eyes and silently told him that he would take this up another time if the Jenners were so inclined. Jenner looked uncertain for a moment, then nodded to his boys. They filed out, boots thumping across the porch.

Sighing deeply, Jim Quartermain said, "Carrie, a man's pride is supposed to be a very tender thing. According to the rules I should resent your interfering and rush out into the street to fight the Jenners, but I'm honest enough to admit I'm relieved to get out of it."

She smiled, relieved, yet worried. "But there *will* be another time, won't there? I only brought you a postponement."

"Yes," he said simply, and went upstairs for her bags.

In the dark alley behind McKeogh and Shipley's Store, Quartermain loaded her baggage on top of the barbed wire and helped her to the high seat. Her long skirts were a hindrance and she gathered them tightly about her legs. Cimarron had tied Quartermain's horse to the tailgate, so all he had to do was cluck to the team and get them moving.

The Jenners were sitting their horses along the darkened street as Quartermain drove out. Horace Pendergast stepped out of the shadows of the harnessmaker's store, and the Jenners all swung around to look at him. Pendergast touched a match to his cigar; the momentary flare revealing his blocky face.

He said, "Quartermain made a damn fool out of you, didn't he? I never thought I'd see the day."

"There's another time coming," Rob Jenner said in his bass rumble.

"He put you on the run once. He'll do it again," Pendergast said. "That's Ben Bickerstaff's boy, Rob, and what Bickerstaff didn't teach him, Lee did. You'll go some to find a man who can beat him to the draw and shoot."

"I'm not afraid of him," Parker said.

"Takes more than courage," Pendergast said. He turned his head to Rob Jenner. "You'll never whip Quartermain, not the way you fight. You're too honest."

"What are you trying to say?"

"One of two things. Either get a man who can face him and win—" he paused to puff his cigar "—or get a man who don't mind shooting him in the back."

"Why, now—"

"Just a minute!" Pendergast said sharply. "You have no choice, Jenner. If Quartermain strings that fence, you're cut off from a good winter range. Do you actually think you can make him quit?" Pendergast put just enough laughter into his voice to make it smart. "You can't and you know it.

He came closer to Rob Jenner's stirrup and spoke in a milder tone. "I have a big stake in the San Saba, Jenner, and I don't want to sit by and watch you blow it away for me."

"So?"

"So there happens to be a couple of men in town who are working for me. They can do you a lot of good. I'll send them out in the morning."

"What kind of men?" Rob Jenner asked.

"Don't go proud on me," Pendergast said. "Jenner, you'll do this my way or you won't have any range left in three months."

"I got no cash to hire men," Jenner said.

"Let me worry about the finances," Pendergast said softly. "I have a large stake in this, Rob, so just consider them a loan. Remember, I don't want to get openly involved. We'll keep this between ourselves. I'll send the men out to Long Knife. They'll know what to do."

"Gunfighters?"

Pendergast studied the ash on his cigar. "Let's just say that these men are a little bolder than the average. Suit you?"

"Do I have a choice?"

"Not much," Pendergast admitted, "unless you want to hand everything to Jim Quartermain."

"All right," Jenner said, somewhat reluctantly. "Send 'em out."

He gigged his horse with his heels and they rode from town at a trot.

CHAPTER 7

For an hour Jim Quartermain drove in silence. The dull plodding of the team was the only break in the monotony. Finally Carrie Holderman said, "Crystal City came apart at the seams the night you left, Jim."

"I thought it would."

"Winn Harlow tried to take over the town, but he didn't make it. Dad's vigilantes stepped in and stopped him and his bunch."

Quartermain peered through the darkness at the pale oval of her face. "Dead?"

"No," she said. "But he was beaten badly. He got away from the mob and left town on a fast horse."

"He won't like that," Quartermain said. "The man's pride was the biggest thing about him. I suppose my name is unpopular in Crystal City."

"Very," she said. She took his arm, hugging it against her side and the soft swell of her breast. "Quartermain is a dirty word now. Does it really bother you?"

"A little. A man likes to leave a clean slate behind." He sighed. "What am I going to do with you, Carrie?"

"Marry me." She tried for a certain lightness, but it did not come off. Her desire was too strong, her longing too real for joking.

56

"Nothing has changed," Quartermain said. "I'm sorry, Carrie."

She sat quietly for a moment. "Jim, are you in love with someone else?"

"No," he said. "I'd know if I were and I'd tell you."

"I'm not so sure," she said, and when he flipped his head around, she added, "About knowing, I mean. Some things are always hidden from us." She grew thoughtful. "What about Jane Beal? You've told me a lot about Andy and Izee, but never Jane. I suppose this is one of the small things women are supposed to pick on, but I've always wondered if she meant something special to you. Did she, Jim?"

"Yes," he admitted honestly. "Once she did." He fired a cigar, his face grave in the brief flare of the match. "But that's all over. She's older now. Grown up and forgotten about it."

"But you did love her?"

"I don't know," Jim Quartermain said. "What does a man of twenty know about love?" He puffed his cigar for a moment. "I haven't seen Jane since she was sixteen, Carrie. I don't know what she'll be like now, but once we were very close. Blame it on the fact that we were both young and wanted to find out what life was all about. I know of no other way to express it."

"I see," Carrie said. "I thought it was something like that, but I always had the foolish notion that it was the woman who felt guilty afterward."

"Carrie, we were children! It's not the same."

"That's what you keep saying. Yet you remember. So what's the difference?"

Quartermain didn't know what the difference was. He butted his cigar against the wagon box and threw the dead shards into the grass near the roadside.

"Jim, the reason you wouldn't marry me—was it because you were afraid that someday you'd see Jane again and the old feeling would all come back? Were you afraid you'd find out that you didn't love me enough and then be sorry?"

"Something like that," he admitted. He pulled the team to a halt and wrapped the reins around the brake handle. Taking her by the shoulder he half turned her toward him. "Carrie, I never wanted to hurt you. But if we did marry and then I had to face something like that, you'd be hurt. We couldn't hide the truth from each other."

"I know that," she said, and turned her head away from him. He unwrapped the reins from the brake and drove on.

"I've made a prime fool of myself, haven't I?" Her voice was deep and controlled. "Coming here. Following you like an impulsive school girl. I was thinking of orange blossoms and an organ playing soft music. You must really be laughing at me, Jim."

"Carrie, why are you doing this to yourself?" He saw the words run off her mind and he fell silent. What could he say to her? Could he tell her that she alone made his nights more lonely and unbearable? How could he separate in his mind the genuine love that she deserved and what he felt for her? He had to be sure, and because he was not, he held himself in severe check.

He said, "I'll have Gil take you into town in the morning and see that you get on the stage."

She remained silent so long that he thought she accepted this and the fact that she did caused him a sharp regret. "No," she said. "I'm going to stay. I want to meet her, Jim. She's used weapons on you that I haven't, and if I have to fight for you, then I don't want to be denied anything."

She reached across to the reins and pulled the team to a halt. Then she twisted on the seat and leaned back across his lap. Her arms came up around his neck and her lips searched until they found his. She had never kissed him like this before, but now she showed him the full depth of her love. There was that essence of the gambler in her, a controlled boldness that allowed her to take a chance other women would have avoided. She pulled her lips away from his when she felt him lose the grip on his hungers and she leaned against him, emotion dying within them like ripples on a quiet pool.

"You see," she said. "I can do that too. Any pretty woman can do that to a man, Jim." Then her determinaton faltered and her faith parted for a moment and she had to ask, "Was it the same, Jim? Was there no difference?"

He whispered against her hair, "I don't want to compare you to anyone, Carrie. You can see why I have to be sure. You wouldn't want me any other way."

58

"No," she said, and sat upright on the seat. "I wouldn't want you any other way."

Jim Quartermain looked at her in the darkness, trying to retain some grip on the moment passed, but it was gone beyond recall. He picked up the reins and clucked the team into motion.

Held back by the heavy load and slow pace, they didn't pull into the ranch yard until almost midnight. A small lamp glowed in the bunkhouse and another in the parlor.

Gil Purvis pranced aross the porch and offered Carrie a hand down. Cimarron came across the yard on the run and led the team and wagon to the barn. Purvis had made himself at home and he took Carrie's baggage to Andy's old room. She followed him down the hall, and when Purvis came back, Quartermain was seated in the parlor.

"Man," Purvis said, "just smell that clean Texas air." He shot Quartermain an amused glance, checking the darkening bruises on his cheeks. "Feelin' pretty tough in the hotel lobby, wasn't you?"

"Maybe," Quartermain said. "Rob Jenner understood that a lot better than words."

"Damned curly wolf," Purvis said with some admiration. "You think he'll fight?"

"He's never turned one down," Quartermain said. "He's made his talk and now he'll back it."

"Big-mouthed fool! Ornery old windbag! He'll cuss the undertaker for not layin' him out proper." Boots rattled across the porch and Purvis closed his mouth with a snap when Cimarron came in.

Quartermain said, "Get the crew together at daybreak. We're going to string wire."

Cimarron grunted. "You don't let any grass grow under your feet, do you?"

"Am I supposed to? See that the men are armed with rifles and have Cookie load up a wagon to take along. We'll leave a guard with each piece of fence that goes up."

"That's askin' for a fight," Cimarrron said.

"Dammit," Quartermain snapped, "you want to give orders or take them around here?"

"Allrightallright," Cimarron said, and went back to the bunkhouse.

"What's he sore about?" Purvis asked.

"Ask him."

"I may just do that," Purvis said, and yawned hugely. "I think I'll turn in—" he grinned "—Boss."

"Go to hell," Quartermain said. He watched Purvis leave, then blew out the lamp and made his way down the dark hall to Izee Beal's room. He scratched a match, got the lamp working and took off his coat and shirt.

Quartermain removed his gun harness before he sat on the edge of the bed. He felt bone tired and the whole side of his face ached. Raising a hand, he touched the bruise and found that he needed a shave.

To hell with that too, he thought, and tugged off his boots. He turned out the lamp and lay back, folding his arms across his face.

Quartermain was up and dressed before the dawn light sneaked into his room. He took his breakfast in the cook-shack with the crew, wearing faded levis and blue shirt, a rag-tag cowhide vest and a pair of elkhide shotgun breeches. He was not wearing his gun when he sat down at the long table. Nine pairs of eyes rose over the plates and gave him a quick glance.

Other than Purvis and Cimarron, these men were strangers, but this did not surprise him. The West was full of drifters, men who worked a season and rode away. They were a restless lot and stability of temperament was not a cowboy's strongest trait.

He made it a point to finish his meal first. He stood up. The others were taking their time, purposely stalling to see what he would do. He touched Cimarron on the shoulder and said, "Get them outside and ready for work in five minutes."

"You get 'em out," Cimarron said. "They're still eatin'."

Quartermain looked around the table and found them watching him, a vague amusement in their eyes. Suddenly he reached for the edge of the table and upended it with a jarring crash. Food and dishes scattered on the floor and in laps. Men cursed and fought to get away from this tipping mess and when they were all standing, Quartermain said, "You're through eating now. I can take you one at a time and whip you, but you look smarter than that. Five minutes, I said, and if I was you, I wouldn't be late."

This was a bad moment and Quartermain knew it. He was asking for trouble and if they all jumped him at once,

60

neither Purvis nor Cimarron would come to his rescue. Everyone knew the rules and he was ready to play.

The men saw this and measured him. Then one man grinned and said, "I'm full anyhow," and walked out. The others followed him to the corral where they cut out horses. Purvis sighed like a man relieved from a terrible strain and Cimarron shook his head in silent respect.

"I would never have done that," he said. "There's some tough men working here."

"The tougher the better," Quartermain said, and went back to the house.

Exactly five minutes later they assembled outside in the first pink rays of the sun. The wire wagon came up and the crew sat their horses, waiting. Quartermain and Cimarron led them out while Gil Purvis brought up the rear.

Through the day, Quartermain drove the crew hard. Strands of new wire glistened like silver thread in the sunlight. The heat mounted and men sweated and horses raised thick, choking dust around them. At sundown, Quartermain left two men behind to split a guard shift.

Riding back to the ranch, Cimarron complained of this. "You can't push men hard all day like this and then expect 'em to stand guard half th' night."

Quartermain regarded Cimarron closely for a moment. "Would you rather have it cut during the night and string it all over tomorrow?"

"Forget I mentioned it," Cimarron said. He spurred his horse on ahead, and Purvis dropped back to ride beside Quartermain.

"Perky gent, ain't he?"

"He's tired."

"We're all tired, but we ain't discontented. He is."

"You never liked him, did you?" Quartermain looked at his friend.

"Can't rightly say's I ever did," Purvis admitted. "Course, he ain't never done me no harm, either."

"Keep off his back," Quartermain warned. "Cimarron's tough."

Purvis laughed softly. "Well now, I've done a little squintin' at the elephant myself."

"Difference there," Quartermain said. "Cimarron squints over a gun barrel."

At the ranch, he turned his horse out and washed at

the well before going into the house. He heard Carrie in the kitchen, but went into the parlor instead. Izee's desk sat in the corner and Quartermain rolled back the top and pulled out the record that told the life and death story of a ranch in irregular columns of figures.

For nearly an hour he added and balanced on an old piece of wrapping paper. Then he heard Carrie's footsteps in the hall. She came in and sat on the edge of the desk. She wore a print dress with full sleeves and he could see the outline of her tapered legs beneath the cloth.

"Did you have to leave like that this morning?" she asked.

He stroked his mustache with his forefinger. "You ought to wear more petticoats."

She laughed and smoothed the dress over her legs. "Too hot. I won't stand with the sun behind me, if that's worrying you."

He laughed suddenly and threw the pencil stub aside. She could take him during a most troubled state of mind and raise him out of it without effort. This was her gift, a natural optimism that affected him strongly. Almost everything in life pleased her, gave her happiness, and she transferred it to him.

"Carrie," he said seriously, "put a lock on your door."

"Do I need one, Jim?"

"I don't know. But the moment you'd find out whether you did or not would be too late."

She put her palm against his cheek and scraped his whiskers. "You need a shave, but I like you this way. For the first night in over two years I slept without hearing a gun go off. You don't know how nice that was."

"Guns can go off here too."

"It would be different here." She cupped his face in her palms for a kiss. When she pulled away, she said, "I baked you a peach pie."

"You campaigning, Carrie?"

She shook her head. "I don't campaign, Jim. You know what I am. A year, a day, wouldn't change anything." She slid off the desk and went back into the kitchen. He listened to the small sounds she made, a rattle of a pan, the shuffle of the stove grates. Then he went back to his books.

It was after nine when he finished. Carrie had brought

him a wedge of pie and this was his supper. Quartermain was not thinking of food when he closed the desk and walked across the yard to the bunkhouse. He opened the door and looked around. Purvis was on his bunk reading a yellow-back novel. Quartermain touched one of the Running W riders and said, "You on the roundup when Izee sold off?"

"Sure," the man said and snubbed out his cigaret. "All of us were."

The men in the bunkhouse listened carefully. Only Gil Purvis went on reading, his lips moving slowly as he spelled out the words.

"Who ramrodded it?"

"Cherokee was boss," the man said. "Cimarron handled the beef sale in Abilene while the old man and Cherokee took the train east after shorthorns."

"Where's Cimarron now?" Quartermain asked.

"Don't know." The man lay back on his bunk. "He comes and goes pretty much to suit himself."

"I heard him ride out an hour ago," Purvis said, not taking his eyes from his page.

"Thanks," Quartermain said, and went back to the house. Carrie Holderman was on the porch and she followed him inside.

"I heard you slam out. What's the matter, Jim?"

"Nothing," he said shortly. Then he stopped and took her arm, speaking more gently. "Nothing, Carrie. Don't worry about me. I'll be back by morning."

"Morning? But where—"

"I don't know where," Quartermain said. "If Cimarron comes back before I do, tell Purvis quietly that I want him to hang around until I get back. You understand?"

"Yes," Carrie said, and Quartermain went to his room for his gun.

Gil Purvis was waiting by the corral, and he had saddled Quartermain's horse. Quartermain said, "You read minds?"

"Wasn't hard to figure out," Purvis said. "You read somethin' in the books you didn't like. Fella does that now and then. You might say there was a slip of the pencil. Makes life real complicated for a man if he don't watch himself."

"You through with your homespun philosophy?"

Quartermain mounted and left the yard, riding toward the section of fence which the crew had completed that day.

While he rode through the darkness, Quartermain reviewed the small errors that finally had stood out so glaringly. He had recognized Izee Beal's writing and Cherokee's almost illegible scrawl, but here and there erasures had been made and the totals doctored. Since Cimarron was in some authority on the Running W, Quartermain selected him as the man to get the answers from.

Approaching the fence, Quartermain slowed his horse to a walk, but he did not stop until a voice said, "That's far enough!"

"Quartermain," he said, and stepped from the saddle. He scratched a match and put a light on himself. Shadows moved and a man lowered his rifle. Ground hitching his horse, Quartermain squatted by the bedrolls. One man propped himself up on an elbow.

"Either of you seen Cimarron tonight?"

"Nope," one said. He was little more than a kid and he made a show of rolling a smoke, popping a match to it. "He ain't been around. You want us to tell him somethin' should we see him?"

"No. I'll tell him myself," Quartermain said. He remounted again. "What's out there now?" He pointed to a row of low hills that fell off to the river land.

"Nesters."

"Thanks," Quartermain said, and rode off into the night.

The two men listened to the fading sounds. Then one stuck two fingers in his mouth and whistled softly.

Cimarron came up quietly and knelt by the bedrolls. "You did real fine, boys. I'll see that you're thanked proper next time we're in town."

"What you into?" the skinny one asked.

"Just never you mind," Cimarron said. "What you don't know won't hurt you. You never seen me at all tonight. Remember that."

"Sure," the thin cowboy said, and Cimarron walked over to his picketed horse. He mounted up and rode away, in the same general direction of Jim Quartermain, had taken.

Farther ahead, Quartermain waited in a juniper thicket, his hand over the horse's nostrils. He listened with his head cocked to one side until he picked up the soft plop of a hoof in dust. A moment later the rider passed within

64

ten feet of him, a vague outline, but Quartermain recognized Cimarron.

He smiled, waited a while then mounted and followed at a walk. He had suspected that his crew would lie to him because he was a stranger to them yet. Given a month, he would have got the truth, but now they were loyal to the old men and Cimarron had been their boss for some time.

Quartermain settled himself to a steady pace and an hour later he entered the first slope of the hills. He rode more alertly now, for the land was beginning to rough up and he could easily overtake Cimarron, an event that might prove disastrous.

He felt sure that he had not lost the man, however, for he could still smell dust strongly in this still night air, a sure sign that the rider moved on ahead. But once in the hills, the trail began to work through wooded land and the smell of dust petered out.

For an hour Quartermain trailed by guess and by instinct, then broke out on a narrow winding path that led over a ridge and into a short valley. Midnight found him traversing a swale that let down toward the outline of a nester's cabin in a wooded hollow.

A bright light shone through the cabin window, so Quartermain tied his horse in the timber and went on afoot. He made a circuit of the place and came up by way of the outbuildings. He paused at a three-sided horse barn and smiled when he found Cimarron's horse.

Waiting, Quartermain hunkered down against some stacked hay and let the minutes drag into an hour. Finally the cabin door opened—he could see the outflung bar of light—and he left his hiding place and skirted around the other side.

Flattened against the wall, he head Cimarron's low murmur and a woman's answering laugh. Then Cimarron went around the other side and got his horse from the lean-to. The woman stood in the doorway, looking toward the rise of hills, then turned to go back inside. Quartermain moved quickly and caught the door just as it was about to close. The woman opened her mouth to cry out and Quartermain shoved her, sending her stumbling backward into the cabin. He closed the door, slid the bar and leaned against it.

The woman recovered quickly from her fright. She smiled, a mechanical, forced smile calculatd to lure a man. She was young, in her mid-twenties. Once she had been beautiful, but beauty had faded, leaving her skin too pale, her cheekbones raw ridges that made hollows of her cheeks.

She wore the thinnest of dresses and nothing beneath it. She coughed and her breasts were moving pendants beneath the cloth. "This could be a busy night," she said. "Care for a cup of coffee, honey?"

"No," Quartermain said, and watched her turn to the stove. He had seen her kind before, in a thousand isolated places, living alone and making their living the best they could. "What's your name?"

"Call me Trixie." She laughed. "What's in a name?"

"Mine's Quartermain. You got a title to this place?"

"Title?" She poured a cup of coffee and sat down at the table. Her legs were thin and her hipbones sharp. "You own this land or somethin'?" She nodded wisely. "Sure, I get it. You just can't stand to see a girl make an honest dollar. You going to put me off?"

"What was Cimarron doing here tonight?"

"What do you think?" She laughed and pulled her dress up above the knee. "A man gets lonesome, or don't it bother you?"

Quartermain turned to the door and slid the bolt back. "You've got a week to clear out, Trixie."

"Say now—" she began, but Quartermain had gone outside. The girl knocked over her cup of coffee getting to her feet to follow him. She caught him outside and grabbed his arm. "Wait a minute. Can't we talk this over?"

"Talk what over?"

"Talk what over, he says. Sure, that's the way it is with you big men. Spit on people like me, but you'll come around sooner or later." She jabbed Quartermain's chest with her finger. "Listen big man, Running W built this place for me. Labor, love and money. What do you say about that?"

"I've already said it—one week!"

"Well, big man, let's just wait a week and see." She placed her hands on her hips and glared at him. The lamplight behind her silhouetted her through the thin

66

dress. "There's men around here who can pare you down to pan size. Get pushy and you'll—"

She stopped talking suddenly and whipped her glance toward the dark valley leading into this clearing. From a distance, the drum of a running horse was clear in the silence. Almost violently she began to push at Quartermain. "Get out of here! Please! Go now, but hurry."

"Why can't I meet your friend?" Quartermain asked.

"No! There'll be trouble! He's jealous."

Avoiding the light shafting through the partially open door, Quartermain stepped toward the corner of the cabin. The rider was no more than a quarter of a mile away and coming on fast.

"I'll be back in a week," he said, and ran toward the lean-to. Circling the shed, he entered the timber and began to race toward a position that afforded him a clear view of the cabin. He clung to the inky blackness of the trees and watched Parker Jenner dismount and step into the lighted doorway. Trixie reached past him and pulled the door closed while Quartermain went up the hill for his horse.

Perker Jenner helped himself to the coffee and sat down at the table. His face was bruised from the belting his father had given him, but his eyes still contained a bold swagger.

"Quartermain just left here," Trixie said, and giggled when Parker spilled some of his coffee in his lap.

"Just now?"

Trixie nodded. "Two jumps ahead of you." Her smile deepened. "Be careful of him, Parker. He's too good for you."

"There's only one way to find that out," Parker said, forcing himself to relax again. "What did he want?"

"Cimarron. Quartermain suspects something." She moved around the back of Parker's chair and ran her fingers through his thick hair. "You don't come around and see me any more, Parker. I miss you."

"Cut it out." He moved his head aside so that her hand fell away. "What did Cimarron have to say?"

"A section of the fence is up. There's two men guarding it with rifles."

"Then it'll be easy," Parker said. He stood up. He turned back to the stove, and instead of walking around her, he bumped her in the chest with his elbow, pushing her aside.

"Quartermain gave me a week to get out," Trixie said. "Don't you care, Parker?"

"Why should I?" He lifted the pot, shook what was left in it, then threw it on the plank floor. Coffee spread in a wide stain and the lid rolled beneath her brass bed. "Hell, you can't even make good coffee!"

She bit her lip and watched him. "Parker, why do you do this to me?"

His head came around and he stared at her, daring her to defy him. "Do what?"

"Treat me like dirt?"

He laughed. "Well? What are you?"

"I was good enough for you before you began foolin' around McKitrich's wife! What do you think's goin' to happen when he finds out?"

"Shut your mouth!" he snapped, his eyes blazing.

His anger died as quickly as it had flared up, and he said, "You want me to tell Pendergast?"

"I guess you better," she said. "Parker, don't let Quartermain send me away. Let me stay." She sat down at the table and ran her fingers through her hair and tried to smile. "When I was a little girl I used to think of a home of my own and a man and kids. That seems like such a long time ago."

"For you it was."

She raised her eyes quickly and watched him. "You like to hurt me, don't you? Is it because I'm weak and dumb and you despise that in any woman? I suppose you would because you're that way yourself. You'd want a strong woman, but none of them would have you. You got McKitrich's wife fooled, Parker, but she'll get ashamed one of these days and then you'll come back here to me. You always do."

He smiled wryly and stepped toward her. Fisting her hair, he pulled her head back sharply and cocked his fist to strike. His grip hurt her and tears came into her eyes, but she regarded him with a calm fatalism.

"I could make that skinny face so funny no man would want you with a blanket thrown over it," he said. "You want me to do it?"

68

"I don't care," she said. "I just don't care about anything any more."

Had she raised her voice or exhibited fear, his temper would have unleased like a spring, but her coolness kicked the props from beneath his pride. He saw her as a woman more courageous than he would ever be, for she could admit her own weaknesses, a thing he could not do.

He released her hair and turned toward the door, pausing there. "I'll see that Pendergast knows about Quartermain."

He went outside and mounted his horse. Trixie came to the door, watched him ride away, then turned back. She did not lock her door because she had no fear of anyone. Her bed was in the far corner and she got down on her hands and knees to get the coffee pot lid.

The coffee had soaked into the wood, leaving a dark stain, and she looked at this untidy spot as though it symbolized some deep stain on her soul.

By her bed stood a scarred dresser and a mirror supported by a nail driven into the logs. She slipped out of her dress, letting it fall in a limp heap at her feet, then studied herself in the mirror. Her image returned to her, gaunt, bony, the flesh no longer firm with the bloom of youth.

Aloud she said, almost in anguish, "I *am* young!"

Her voice was an alien sound in the empty room, and then she pressed her hands over her eyes to shut out the image in the mirror. Her crying began as a soft, lost sobbing. Lost because there was no one beside herself to hear it.

CHAPTER 8

A few minutes before eleven, Cherokee Nye wheeled into the yard with the buggy and then dismounted to hand Jane Beal to the ground. The foreman bundled her luggage under his arms and in each hand and followed her up the porch steps.

Jane saw a lighted lamp in the parlor and paused in the arch, her head cocked to one side. Carrie Holderman lay on the horsehair sofa, one arm tucked beneath her head, sound asleep.

Stripping off her gloves and hat, Jane walked softly into the room to stand near Carrie, looking down at her. Jane was not tall, but nature had designed her full body to catch men's eyes. She wore her reddish-blond hair in a bun on the back of her head. Her eyes were veiled by long lashes and in the lamplight, almost green.

She looked Carrie over from head to foot, then said, "Whoever she belongs to has damned good taste."

Cherokee reddened and shifted his feet and Carrie came awake. She rubbed her eyes and sat up, looking at Jane Beal. "I'm sorry," she said. "I must have fallen asleep. You're Jane, aren't you?"

"I know who I am," Jane said. "Who are you? The housekeeper?"

Cherokee said hurriedly, "She sure as hell wasn't here when I left."

Carrie got up and smoothed her dress. "I'm Jim Quartermain's guest. Carrie Holderman. I've been looking forward to meeting you, Jane."

"Have you?" Jane's eyebrow ascended slightly and then she turned away. "Put my luggage away, Cherokee. I'll stay here and chat with Jim's, ah—guest." Cherokee hefted the bags again and seemed eager to leave. Jane Beal walked around the room, touching the backs of chairs. Finally she whirled with a lifting of skirts and met Carrie's eyes with a frank displeasure. "Where is Jim?"

"Out," Carrie said. "He left around nine and said he'd be back in the morning."

"I see. How long do you plan to stay, Miss Holderman?"

"Permanently," Carrie said, and watched the surprise break the mask of Jane Beal's beauty. *I have claws too, honey!*

Jane smiled and said sweetly, "But that is such a long time, darling. Don't you think it's going to be a little crowded?"

"I don't think so," Carrie said. "If Jim leaves, of course I'd leave with him." She sat down again and folded her hands demurely in her lap, "You're just like he described you," she said, "except perhaps—older."

70

Jane Beal flexed her fingers like a bird sharpening his claws on a hardwood limb. "Jim was never very practical when it came to women," she said. "He's easily misled."

"He told me you discovered that at an early age," Carrie said.

"Really! I—" Jane kicked her anger in place. "I'm very tired. Perhaps we can discuss it tomorrow when we both feel better." She gathered her hat and gloves and moved to the hallway, pausing there to look back at Carrie. "We're not going to like each other at all, are we?"

"Did you think we would?" Carrie asked.

She smiled as Jane went down the lamplit hall with a swirl of skirts, but the smile faded quickly. She bit her lower lip, said, "Damn, but she's beautiful," and suddenly felt exhausted. She lay down again, and when Cherokee came through the house a moment later, she seemed to be asleep.

Joel McKitrich found that sleep was impossible, so he got up, lighted the lamp and fried himself an egg. He had built well: his cabin had two rooms with the partially completed wall of a third. Every time he looked at his place he told himself that he had done well in three years.

His wife got up, opening the bedroom door that separated the two rooms. She was young, no more than nineteen, with full breasts and flaxen hair. McKitrich turned his head and looked at her.

"Couldn't sleep," he said, sliding his egg onto a plate.

"I heard you stirrin'," she said. "You been restless since the funeral."

"I'm not bothered," he told her. "They're not our troubles. A man don't have to get involved unless he wants to, and I don't want to." He made a lifting motion with his plate. "You want some?"

She shook her head and moved around the table. The lamplight was behind her, shining through the thin cotton nightgown, and he could see her as clearly as if she were naked. He stared at the tapered lines of her legs until they lost themselves in the darker shadows of her hips, and a small muscle flickered along his jaw.

He went outside to eat his egg.

The night was cool with a breeze blowing up from the river. In the distance he heard the faint running pound of a horse and listened carefully. His wife came out and stood by him, listening too.

"Comes by here pretty regular," McKitrich said. "Always in a hurry. I wonder what's waiting for a man to make him hurry so." He glanced up at her. She had her arms clasped tightly across her full breasts. The nightgown was drawn smooth over her rounded hips. McKitrich pulled his eyes away and finished his egg.

I'm twice her age, he thought, and in his mind then came an almost overpowering regret that he had married her, for in his point of view, marriage to him had cheated her. In many ways she was a little girl with a great love of laughter, while all that had long ago been taken from him, leaving him silently thoughtful and faintly taciturn.

McKitrich put his plate aside and stood up, slipping his arm around the softness of her waist. Beneath his fingers, her stomach muscles tightened slightly, then relaxed. He said, "Ella, do you have any regrets?"

She tilted her head to look at him and light fell on her full lips. "Regrets? I don't think so."

"I haven't been what you wanted," McKitrich said. "You should have married a laughin' man, Ella. A man who liked to play the fiddle."

"I've never complained," she said. "You shouldn't trouble yourself over it, Joel."

He hooked his finger beneath her chin and brought her face around to his. "You're an uncommonly pretty girl, Ella. I guess I don't tell you that often enough, but I feel it."

"I know. I'm not thirstin' for sweet talk."

"What do you thirst for then?"

"Nothin' we don't have," she said, and moved to turn away from his hands. "Better come in now."

"Wait," he said, holding her arm. "Ella, it wasn't worry that kept me awake." His voice grew deep with half hidden hungers. "Golly, but you can make a man dangle."

She regarded him levelly, without love and without hate. "All right, if that's what you want." She went into the house and did not close the bedroom door behind her.

Joel McKitrich followed her with his eyes, then stood

72

there, half angry, and sharply hurt. He was learning to hate the calm acceptance in her voice. Sometimes he wished she would fight him, strike him.

But she never did that. She just said, "If that's what you want," and left him with that feeling of half shame, as if he were a demanding man.

McKitrich sighed and closed the outer door before snuffing out the lamp. He went back into the bedroom, and in the total silence he heard her even breathing in the darkness.

Quartermain returned to his own ranch house near daybreak, swung off by the barn and turned his horse into a stall. Several hands lounged near the cook shack, early risers making sure they had first pull at the coffee pot. Quartermain walked across the dry and caked yard to the house.

Dawn was rinsing the darkness away and the distant outlines of the land became clearer. Crossing the porch, he went into the parlor and poured himself a drink from the whiskey bottle Izee always kept in the desk. The burning in his stomach flooded him with momentary warmth and some of the ache in his legs left him. He felt dirty and tired and the whiskers on his face were half an inch long, matted with sweat and dust.

Cherokee Nye thumped across the porch and paused in the dooway.

"See you got back," Quartermain said, "Good trip?"

"Passable," Nye said, and slumped in a chair. "You doin' some night ridin'?"

"Some," Quartermain said. "Cimarron come back yet?"

"Come and gone," Cherokee said.

Quartermain cursed and slapped his thigh. "Dammit. why didn't you hold him?"

"What for? What's he done? You expect me to know everything that's goin' on around here?"

"Yes," Quartermain snapped. "You draw foreman's wages. You better start earnin' them."

"Now wait a minute—" Cherokee began, but Quartermain shoved open the desk top and withdrew the books. He opened them and said, "You make these entries?"

"Most of 'em," Cherokee admitted, not even glancing at the ledgers.

73

"Look at them!" Quartermain commanded. "Don't be so damned smart you think you couldn't make a mistake!"

Cherokee's eyes showed a flaring resentment, but he took the books and scanned the columns.

"Did Cimarron make this erasure?" Quartermain asked, pointing.

"Must have. I never erased nothin'. Neither did Izee that I know of."

"Did you check these figures with the shipper at Abilene? Or the loading pen crew?"

"No, I didn't," Cherokee muttered. "Hell, Cimarron's been here a long time and I thought—"

"That he was honest?" Quartermain tossed the books back in the desk and slammed the top down. "Cherokee, I want that man!"

"All right," Cherokee said, "if you want him that bad I can take a couple of the crew and go after him."

"Keep the crew stringing wire," Quartermain ordered. "I'll find Cimarron." He rummaged in his shirt pocket for a cigar and got it going. "Jane sleeping?"

"Yeah," Cherokee said. "That other woman was a surprise. They sized each other up like a couple stray cats. That Jane's got what it takes. You could see she was all choked up about her pa and Andy, but she wouldn't bust loose with a tear."

"She never cried much," Quartermain said, and Cherokee went out to get the crew ready for work. Daylight was growing more full when he went into the kitchen. He stoked the stove and put on a pan of water for the coffee. From another part of the house he heard someone stir and a moment later Carrie Holderman came in, her hair in braids and a dark robe wrapped tightly around her.

"Jane's here," she said.

"Cherokee told me," Quartermain said, hearing another door open and close. Footsteps padded down the hall and Carrie's face settled into inexpressiveness. She moved past him to tend the coffee pot, keeping her back to the kitchen door as Jane Beal came in.

She paused in the doorway. Her eyes were too large for her face but they gave her a completely innocent expression that contradicted the mature set of her lips. She walked directly toward Jim Quartermain and then threw

74

her arms around him. Some restraining dam broke and she began to cry while he held her.

Carrie Holderman walked out of the room.

Gently Jim Quartermain disengaged Jane's arms and seated her at the table. She sat there, her hands stroking her arms, her lower lip caught between her teeth. Finally she brushed her tears away and said, "I'm sorry, Jim. I guess I don't very often cry, but when I do, I turn on the waterworks."

"You don't have to apologize to anyone," he said "He was thinking of you at the end, Jane."

"I came as quick as I could," she said, and grasped his hands tightly. "Jim, I'm so lost, so alone now."

"You're not alone, Jane. I gave Izee my promise that I'd stay here until there's no more trouble. He changed the will back. You knew about that, didn't you?"

She nodded, and for a moment she avoided his eyes. "I'm not a very good person, Jim." She saw that he was going to deny this and held up her hand. "Let me finish. When you left with Lee, I guess it was my fault. I didn't want you to have any of Running W, Jim. I was too selfish. When Izee cut you out, it was my doing, not because he wanted to."

"That's in the past, Jane."

"No. It's got to be cleared here and now. I can't live with this a minute longer." She curled her fingers around his as though she needed this support. "Because I was small, I wanted half instead of just a third. All right, I got half, but I lost you, Jim. You went away."

"Not because of that, Jane," Quartermain said.

"You still went away," she insisted. "Jim, you don't know how lost I was without you. I came back from school twice. The last time I asked Izee to change his will back, to include you again because it was your right."

"I didn't come back for the land, Jane."

"No, you didn't. That's like you, Jim, ready to do something for someone even if they don't have it coming." Jane lowered her eyes and ran her fingernail along the grain of the wood table. "Why did you promise Izee, Jim? For him or for me?"

"For you," he said honestly. "We've got some unfinished business between us, Jane. I like to keep all the tag ends tied up."

"Are you in love with me?" She looked at him then.

"No," he said. "That was kid's love, Jane."

"Are you in love with her?" She made a motion toward the hall with her head.

"I think I am," he admitted. "Does that hurt, Jane?"

"Almost as much as Izee and Andy dying," she said, "but I don't believe you are, Jim. What is she doing here? Did you bring her here just to hurt me?"

"No," he said. "She came with Gil Purvis. You have to know Carrie to understand her. She wants me to marry her. She believes it's right for us. I believe that too, Jane, but somehow I can't go through with it. You understand?"

She smiled then. "Jim, you're remembering and I like it. Don't ever forget what we were to each other."

He shook his head in silent disagreement. "We're not for each other. We're a chemistry that just won't mix without exploding, Jane. That was one of the reasons I went with Bob Lee. We were heading for destruction and dragging each other down."

"That's where I want to go then," she said, "if it means going with you. Jim, have you considered the fact that we're not just people any longer? We're RunningW, you and I. We could rule the San Saba, Jim. We're strong and the riches go to the strong."

"I guess I'm not after that any more," he said, and got up to move the coffee to the back of the stove. She left her place at the table and came up to him, putting her arms around him.

"You haven't kissed me yet," she said. She canted her head to one side, regarding him. "Afraid, Jim? Afraid that you'll find out you don't love Carrie?"

"I'm not afraid of that," he said, and lowered his lips. She met him freely, her arms tightening. Finally their lips parted and he turned away to pour his coffee. She watched him spill some of it and smiled.

He went back to the table and sat hunched over, his hands around the cup. Jane Beal stood behind his chair and leaned over him with her cheek against his. "Jim, this is terrible to say, but if it took the death of Izee and Andy to bring us together again, then I'm glad it happened." She kissed him lightly. "Get some rest."

He did not answer her and she went down the hall to her room. After he finished his coffee he debated whether

76

he should get some sleep or not. Finally he decided against it. After washing his face in the sink, he went to the corral and roped a fresh horse.

He spent the rest of the morning supervising the stringing of wire. His plan called for fencing two sections at a time, with interlocking gates. At noon he took his meal with the crew, then lay in the shade of the chuckwagon and slept for an hour. Just before sunset he detailed another man to remain behind and followed the crew home. At the barn he caught Cherokee and said, "Put Purvis in Cimarron's place. He'll make a good segundo."

"You sure you want it that way?"

"The way I tell you is the way I want it," Quartermain said, and went to the house. Jane was in the parlor. She gave him a smile, but he went on through the hall to the kitchen. He found Carrie working over the stove and he blew hair away from the back of her neck to kiss her.

"Why can't you let the cook fix the meals?" he asked her.

"I like to do it," she said. Her smile was somewhat reserved as though she were uncertain about him. "I'm out of place here. Maybe I should move into the bunkhouse with the hands."

"You're not funny," he said harshly.

He lathered his face at the sink, stropped the razor that had once been Izee's and removed his whiskers. He was drying his face when Jane came into the kitchen and sat down at the table.

"Jim, tomorrow I want to go to town and check our condition at the bank."

"All right," he said in a half interested voice. "I'll have Cherokee hitch up the buggy and drive you."

"I want you to come along," Jane said. "Cherokee's a hired hand, when it comes right down to it. You're part owner of Running W, and the financial condition of the ranch should be as important to you as it is to me." She got up and moved toward the hall. "I'm sure Carrie understands, don't you, Carrie?"

"Perfectly," Carrie said without turning around.

After Jane went back to the parlor, Quartermain said, "Aren't you two getting along?"

Carrie gazed at him, amazed. "Jim, that's a foolish

77

question. When two women want the same man, they *never* get along."

"I think you're stretching this way out of shape," Quartermain said. "Jane's half owner. You're forgetting that."

"I'm not forgetting anything!" Carrie snapped, near to tears. "I'm not forgetting that she was first with you and I was second. How can I forget it with her around here to remind me?"

Quartermain stood up and took her by the shoulders, drawing her away from the stove. He untied her apron and threw it across the back of a chair. "Let's go take a walk," he said.

"No!" She tried to pull away from him. "Jim, the dinner'll burn!"

"Then let it burn," he said, and guided her out the back door and around the side of the house. They walked slowly past the barn and corral. From across the flats the smell of hot earth blended with the nitrogen of horses and the manure pile.

A quarter mile behind the barn, they came to the enclosed pasture that held the Herefords. The cattle moved around in the new darkness, vague brown and white shapes. Carrie leaned against the fence and watched them for a while.

"I make you nervous, don't I, Jim?"

"Sometimes," he admitted. "It's just that you—you try to lead me by the hand, Carrie. I don't think I can get used to that."

"It's because I love you," she said. "That makes a person think they know everything, even what's good for another person. Like I think I'm good for you. I've made a mistake coming here, haven't I?"

"Yes," he said simply. "I can see now that you should have stayed in Crystal City. What's the matter with me, Carrie? I want you here and yet I don't. What's wrong with me, that I can't make up my mind?"

"You'll have to find that answer," she said and rested her chin in her cupped hands. "I'm a dreamer, Jim. Mostly about you and me. That's my flaw. I get the dreams mixed up with what is real."

He leaned against a pole, licking a cigar into shape. He arched his head round suddenly when he heard a dull

78

pop float across the distance. Then there was another and he threw the cigar down.

"The Jenners are hitting the fence!"

He left Carrie standing there and raced for the bunkhouse, but she hoisted her skirts and ran after him. Some of the crew had been outside when the firing started and were now rushing to catch up their horses.

Purvis yelled, "I'll saddle one for you, Jim!" and Quartermain dashed on to the house for his gun.

When he came out, he found Carrie standing in the dusty yard, watching the men lead horses from the corral. She said, "Now it's guns again."

"Go back to the house," he said gently. "I'll wake you when I get back."

"I won't sleep until you do." She took his arm. "Jim, about Jane—she excites you, doesn't she? All fire and fight—you like that in a woman, don't you?"

"Yes, I like it, but liking it isn't love."

"I suppose not," she said. "But that doesn't mean that you love me either, does it?" She did not wait for his answer, but ran to the house as though she had already guessed it and could not bear to hear him say it. Purvis came up with a horse and Quartermain mounted and led the crew from the yard at a run.

Cherokee and Purvis sided him as they pounded across the flats. The smattering of shooting had died off by the time the Running W crew arrived at the fence line. A fire had been started and the men dismounted to cluster around it. Quartermain's first question was, "Anybody hurt?"

"Bullet shattered my rifle stock," one man said. He came up from the surrounding darkness with the broken gun in his hands. "Jenners' bunch. It was dark as hell and I didn't get a good look at any of 'em, but I'd know Parker's squeaky voice any place."

Someone threw some broken fence posts on the fire and the circle of light spread. A rider stood to one side, punching spent shells from his gun. "Like Chet says, I heard Parker Jenner, but didn't get a close look at any of the others. There was four, though."

Purvis came back from checking the fence. "None of the wire's been cut," he said. "Beats the hell out of me how little damage was done for such a lot of shootin'."

This fact puzzled Quartermain too. He said. "Cherokee,

79

take the crew back. I'm going for a ride and I'll bed down here on the way home. Anyone have an extra blanket on their saddle, leave it here."

Purvis began to grow nervous. "You an't goin' to Long Knife, are you?"

"I'll be safe enough," Quartermain said. "Appears to me that Rob Jenner made this raid to warn us. Sort of a scare. Now it's up to me to show him it didn't work."

"Damn fool," Cherokee said. "Let's take the crew and show him."

"Uh, uh," Quartermain argued. "Men will get killed. Alone, I can ride in and out under a truce." He went to his horse and mounted, moving off immediately. He followed the fence for nearly a mile to where it ended, then cut across the land. He walked the horse and dozed in the saddle, and an hour later he found the road that led to Long Knife.

In the distance he could hear the rattle of a buggy. He pulled off the road. The night was dark, but a man could see for twenty yards and he waited until the shadow of the rig loomed toward him. The driver saw him and lashed the team into a frenzied run. Quite surprised, Quartermain shouted and half blocked the road. But then the buggy swerved and the driver lashed out with his whip, catching Quartermain's horse across the rump and starting it bucking.

There was no chance of pursuit for the horse pitched wildly and for several minutes Quartermain fought the animal with all the skill he possessed. Finally he checked the horse and looked back down the road. The strong odor of dust lingered but the buggy had disappeared.

He went on toward Rob Jenner's place.

CHAPTER 9

Less than a mile away, Quartermain could see the buildings. Light streaked from the windows like beacons and he approached boldly, keeping his horse at a walk. He went under the pole archway that spanned the road and crossed the dusty yard. A man heard him approach and called out to someone in the house. Then the front door opened and a man moved quickly aside to the shadows.

At the tie-rail before the porch, Quartermain dismounted in the light and from somewhere behind him, a man said, "That's good enough! There's a rifle on you."

"You won't need it," Quartermain said, and stepped to the porch. The man standing in the shadows laughed and he recognized Audie the Kid. Rob Jenner appeared then and came to the edge of the porch.

Jenner said, "Take your gun off this man if he's come in peace." Then he re-entered the house and motioned for Quartermain to follow him. Audie the Kid reached from the shadows and opened the door. Inside, he leaned against the frame, a cigarette dangling from his lips.

He said. "So you're Jim Quartermain," and chuckled. "Seems that I was going to draw on you once. That might have been a mistake, mightn't it?"

"Maybe. Would it have been your first?"

"I guess not," Audie admitted, and puffed on his smoke.

Rob Jenner went into the parlor. "In here, Quartermain."

Quartermain stepped into the largest room and stopped, his eyes going immediately to the man across the room. Winn Harlow said, "Jim, friend, it's good to see you again."

Gone were the man's fine clothes. Even his face looked different now. Bruises mottled his cheeks and half-healed scabs covered his lower lip.

Rob Jenner lighted his pipe. Parker sat by the front window, his feet on the sill. Forney and Bushrod were playing Big Casino by the table in the center of the room.

There were no rugs on the floors, no curtains on the windows. Gear was piled high in the corners and dust covered everything. In their womanless house the Jenners had gotten used to squalor. They paid no attention to it.

Quartermain turned his attention back to Winn Harlow. "I heard you had a rough time in Crystal City. I can't say that I'm sorry."

"That's all right," Harlow said softly. He had large eyes and thick wavy hair, but there was meanness in the full curl of his lips, in the way he looked at a man. He smiled and his tortured face twisted unpleasantly. "I figure on getting it all paid back, every damn lick."

"There's your trouble," Quartermain said. "You always want to make sure everyone gets tit-for-tat. In Crystal City you kept a little book full of names, everybody who'd slighted you. Then when you got some money behind you, you got even—until I stopped you."

"But you won't stop me this time," Harlow said. "I lost my shirt because of you, Quartermain. I mean to take the price of it out of your hide."

From behind Quartermain, Audie the Kid said, "Hadn't we better pull his teeth, Mr. Jenner?"

Rob Jenner looked at the Kid, then at Quartermain. "Did you come here to fight, man?"

"To talk," Quartermain said. "Fighting just gets you killed."

Jenner grunted. "Let him keep his gun then."

"I'd do like the Kid says," Harlow put in. "Remember, I know him."

"And *I* know him!" Rob Jenner said. "I'm givin' the orders here and don't any of you forget it."

"Sure, sure," Harlow said, his resentment masked with narrow eyelids. "You do it your way, but don't say I didn't warn you."

"I came over to find out who started the fight with my crew tonight," Quartermain said.

"My son was there," Jenner said. "Also Audie the Kid, Shallak and Davis."

"This your idea, Rob?"

"No," Jenner said. "It was his." He nodded toward Harlow.

Smiling, Harlow said, "They tell me it was a sight. They had your boys hopping. Too bad you had to miss it, Quartermain."

"Maybe the next time I won't," Quartermain said, then turned back to Rob Jenner. "What are we fighting about, Rob? Something personal, or is it actually over the fence?"

For a moment Jenner was genuinely puzzled. "I have nothing personal against you, Quartermain. I've got over Abe."

"Then let's drop this before someone gets hurt bad. You want a gate, then we'll put up a gate. Anything within reason."

Rob Jenner shifted his feet and looked uneasy. Then he said, "I spoke my word and I'll not go back on it. There's no room around me for a wire fence. I told you I wasn't a dreamer. I'm happy the way I am. Let other men change, but I'll be hanged if I want the changes to bother me."

"I guess the talking's done," Quartermain said. He glanced at Parker, who still sat with his feet cocked up on the window sill. "Don't come around the fence again, boy. Associating with men like these—" he waved his hand at Harlow and Audie the Kid— "will just get you killed."

"Or get *you* killed," Parker said. "Quartermain, I ain't forgot Abe. Not by a jugful I ain't."

"All right," Quartermain said resignedly. He went outside to the porch, stopping by the top step. Audie the Kid and Winn Harlow went out with him.

Quartermain's horse was gone.

Harlow laughed and said, "There's no train to get you out of this one, Quartermain."

"Think I'm going to need any?" Quartermain turned his head to include Harlow in his field of vision. The wind of caution blew through Quartermain but he let none of it show. This irked Winn Harlow, for he liked to see fear in a man.

Audie the Kid had eased to the other side of the porch, out of Quartermain's sight, but this caused him no immediate concern. Harlow was the leader here and the Kid would not move until Harlow did.

Leaning against the porch upright, Harlow stripped the band from a cigar. He scratched a match, then held it poised when Rob Jenner came to the doorway. "Get the hell back in there," he said without looking around. After Jenner turned and went away, Harlow said, "I've got you in a pinch, Quartermain. Make you nervous?"

"Two-bit gun sharps never bothered me much," Quartermain said, and watched Harlow's face tighten.

"You're in no spot to get mouthy," Harlow said. "You're not fooling me, Quartermain. I know how you got your reputation. I've seen it done. You wait until a man is scrooched around in his chair and his gun is all tied up, then brace him." He laughed. "I'm usin' it on you now. There's two men and both behind you. Why don't you try your luck?"

"I guess not," Jim said. "You going to make me walk home?"

"Aw, don't hurry off," Harlow pleaded in a mocking voice. "I've missed you these last few days, Jim. You know, when Doc Holderman's vigilantes were on my back, all I could think of was good old Jim Quartermain and how he used to give me a bad time. I told myself then that if I ever got out of this mess I'd look old Jim up and pay him back every damned lick." His voice hardened. "Lift his pistol, Audie."

Quartermain sensed the Kid's movement behind him. When Audie reached with his right hand, Quartermain drew and whirled at the same time. He caught Audie the Kid completely flat-footed, his right hand too far away from his gun to make a good draw.

Bringing his gun around in an arc, Quartermain laid the barrel across the Kid's temple, then snapped a shot at Winn Harlow, who was drawing his own gun even as he dived for cover. Quartermain's shot chipped wood inches from Harlow's cheek and then Harlow was down on his belly by the porch railing.

Whirling after that shot, Quartermain was swallowed by the night before he took four plunging steps. Having no desire to engage in a fight he could not win, he dashed across the dusty yard toward the barn. A man in the bunkhouse yelled and a light shot out the open door. Quartermain veered to the left where horses milled in the corral and then someone shot blindly from the porch. He never knew where the bullet went.

By the barn he paused to listen. Shallak and Davis were by the house now and Winn Harlow was yelling for someone to bring up a lantern. Skirting the barn, Quartermain came out into a small corral and the horses skittered away as he ducked between the bars. He had no time to waste and he knew it. Someone would light a lantern and the crew would spread out, blocking off his escape while he was still afoot.

Working his way through the corral, Quartermain skirted the other side of the barn. He had a fairly clear view of the yard and he slid along the wall until he came to a side door. Entering, he worked his way past the stalls to the front. Near the large door, Parker Jenner's roan stood three-footed and Quartermain hastily slipped on the bridle. Opening the door just enough to ride through, he vaulted onto the horse bareback and rapped him with his heels.

He came from the barn like a shot from a gun, bending low as the horse ran. Shallak and Davis shot together from a position twenty yards apart to block the road. But Quartermain broke through into the night before they could converge and stop him.

There was no pursuit. He hadn't expected any. A few miles from the Jenner house he brought the horse to a walk and traveled at that speed until he came to his fence crew. There he turned Parker's horse loose, saddled one of his own and rode on to the ranch house.

Two lamps still glowed in the hall when he went through the house to the kitchen. On the back of the stove was a partially filled teakettle of water and Quartermain stripped to the waist and washed. He heard a door open and close gently and smiled when Carrie Holderman came in.

She did not speak. She just walked up to him and then they put their arms around each other and stood there. After a moment she moved away from his arms and said, "Would you like something to eat?"

"Yes," he said, "I would."

He stoked the stove for her while she filled the coffee pot. When the fire was hot enough, she fried him a plate of sausage and eggs. She sat down across from him while he ate and when he pushed the plate back to lift his coffee cup, she asked, "What's the Jenners' house like, Jim?"

He looked at her oddly. "Strange question. I don't really know, Carrie. Like nothing, I guess. Just four walls and a roof. Other than keep the wind and rain out, it has no other function."

She pushed her braids aside and massaged the back of her neck. "I can see that going there did you no good, did it?"

"No," he admitted. "If Winn Harlow and the others hadn't been there, I could have talked sense to Rob. He was on the verge of seeing reason."

"Harlow?" She was definitely surprised.

"He's working for the Jenners." Quartermain told her about Audie the Kid and the two others coming in on the train. He went to the stove for a refill on his coffee and came back. "It struck me as strange that Winn got mixed up in this so quick, but then I suppose he came here to settle his score with me, met Audie the Kid and decided the best way to do it was on the Jenner side of the fence."

"But Audie the Kid knew where he was going when he got on the train," Carrie said gently. "Jim, was Rob Jenner hiring before you got here?"

"I don't know. It looks that way, don't it?" He sat with his coffee cup cuddled between his hands, then reached across the table and touched her on the cheek. "Go back to bed, Carrie."

She slid her chair back and replaced it by the table. "Jim," she said, "I love you."

He raised his eyes to her briefly. "I know, Carrie." She waited a moment longer, then her slippers whispered on the floor and she went down the hall to her room. Quartermain finished his coffee and blew out the lamp.

In his own room he undressed and lay on the bed, bone tired, yet alienated from sleep. He folded his hands behind his head and stared at the dark ceiling.

The sun woke him and he sat up, instinctively realizing that he had overslept. The men were already in the cook shack: the noise of clattering silverware and small talk came to him as he hurried across the yard. He took his place at the end of the table and several men grinned at him.

The horse wrangler was a banty-legged little man with a piping voice. He said, "You had yourself a play party last night, but you're a poor horse trader."

Quartermain poured maple syrup over his hotcakes. "I thought I got the best of it. Pretty hard to tell in the dark."

Gil Purvis slid away from the table, said, "Chatter all day if a man'd let you," and stomped out. The rest of the crew followed him. Quartermain finished his meal alone, and when he went outside, the mounts had been saddled and the wagon was moving slowly toward the fence line.

Purvis and Cherokee came over and Purvis crossed his leg over the saddlehorn, busy with a cigarette. "I heard about Parker's horse. A little trouble?"

Quartermain told him about Harlow and the others and Purvis swore softly. "He didn't lose any time huntin' you, did he?"

86

"No." Quartermain glanced at Cherokee Nye. "You have any idea Rob Jenner was hiring toughs?"

"Nope," Cherokee said. "The old bastard, talkin' to cover up his damned underhanded work!"

"Cool off," Quartermain advised. "Get that fence up and leave one more man out there tonight."

He stood there while they rode out and when the line of riders were a mile away, Quartermain walked back to the house and into the kitchen. Carrie Holderman had a buckboard backed against the rear door and was loading the last of the buckets and mops.

"What's that for?" Quartermain asked.

"Tools for general housecleaning," she said. She took her sun bonnet from the kitchen table and put it on, tying the ribbon beneath her chin. "I'm going over to Rob Jenner's place, Jim. I think I can do more with a pie than a man can with a sixshooter."

"Carrie," Quartermain argued gently, "you don't want to go in that boar's nest. Hell, the place hasn't seen a woman for six or seven years."

"Then it's about time some woman has," she said flatly. "Don't argue with me, Jim. It won't get you anywhere. Rob once had a wife and daughters. He said so himself. Then he must be starved for a decent meal."

"I don't want you over there," Quartermain said. "Can't you understand that?"

"I understood it before you said it," Carrie informed him. "Go take Jane to town. She's waiting for you."

"Oh, so that's it." He leaned against the door frame and tried to kiss her, but she pulled her head aside.

"Don't!" she said sharply. "Jim, I love you, but that's never seemed enough. All right, we'll leave it there. When you make up your mind, tell me. Maybe I'll be interested and maybe I won't."

"Going to find yourself another man?" He said this teasingly and the moment it was out, realized that he had made a mistake.

"I won't be hunting, Jim, but if one comes along, then I won't be waiting any longer either." She climbed into the buckboard, and reined away from the porch. Quartermain looked after the retreating rig, then turned back into the house.

Jane came out of her room wearing a pale yellow dress

87

with a matching bonnet. She smiled and looked out the window at the plume of dust raised by Carrie's rig. "I told her she was foolish but she was determined to be neighborly."

"She's stubborn," Quartermain conceded, and went to the barn to hitch up the buggy. He returned in fifteen minutes and handed Jane Beal into the rig.

"I ought to change clothes," he said.

"You look like a working man," she said. "Izee always used to say that the way to impress a banker was to show up in work clothes."

Quartermain lifted the reins and drove out. The heat of the day was beginning to build and dust swirled around them, whipped up by the thin metal tires. Jane Beal took off her bonnet and shook out her hair. She said, "I learned to multiply in school, Jim. Eighteen thousand acres of Herefords will make us both rich." She slanted him a quick glance. "Or don't you want to be rich?"

"I'd rather be able to walk down the street without my gun on."

"That," Jane said, "is something you'll likely never be able to do." She caught his startled expression and added hastily, "I mean, you're the kind of a man who needs trouble. Jim, you don't want some fire and a pair of slippers. Running W is what you want—eighteen thousand acres and a strong woman."

"A woman like you, Jane?"

"Why not? You know me, Jim. Perhaps better than you have a right to know me. You've been thinking about that, haven't you?"

"Yes," he admitted. "Maybe too much."

"I think Izee planned it this way," Jane said. "He always wanted us together. Sometimes I used to wonder if it was because of the ranch or not. We're strong people, Jim. I think he knew that we'd never let it get away."

He took a cigar from his shirt pocket and touched a match to it. "You and Carrie have one thing in common," he said. "Or maybe it's common with all women. You never let a man make up his own mind if you can help it."

"You think I'm pushing you?"

"Aren't you?"

"No," Jane said. "Jim, I don't have to. I remember too

well the day you rode out. You were going to set the world on fire, Jim. That man hasn't changed. Now you tell yourself something else, but it's all a lie and you know it. If you want to be left alone, why did you promise Izee Beal to see this through? You want to know? Because you still can't pass up a good fight."

Having said enough, she settled back in the seat to let him mull it over. He would be denying it to himself, but in the end he would face the facts and then she would have him. She would never have to ask him again.

CHAPTER 10

Carrie Holderman arrived at the Long Knife ranch house around nine and all the Jenners lined up on the porch and watched her get down from the buckboard. Then Bushrod recovered his manners and hurried to help her with the paraphernalia in the back of the rig.

Winn Harlow came from the bunkhouse and stared, his mottled face unfriendly. Carrie waved to him and called, "I see you got out alive! You're a very lucky man!"

Harlow growled something beneath his breath and turned away. Rob Jenner came off the porch with a heavy waddle and said, "Miss, aren't you the young lady of Quartermain's?" One of his eyes was still closed and his lower lip was puffed out of shape.

"Not quite yet," Carrie said. "I haven't completely talked him into marrying me."

Normally she would never have made so blunt an admission, but she had sized up the Jenners as the kind of men who responded only to complete honesty. And she guessed correctly, for Rob Jenner smiled and said, "The man's a fool, that's plain to see." He grew grave then and added, "But you're in the enemy's camp, Miss. There was trouble last night between your brand and mine."

"That was between brands," Carrie said firmly. "Mr. Jenner, I don't think I have any quarrel with you, have I?" He considered this for a moment, then shook his head.

"There now," she said. "You see, we're friends already. I came over to bake you a pie."

"Well now," Jenner began, "we manage pretty fair by ourselves—"

"But I don't mind at all," Carrie said and went into the house. The men followed her in a line and she stopped in the kitchen to survey the mess. Placing her hands on her hips, she said, "I'll have to straighten things out a little first." She turned and took Bushrod and Jethro by the arm. "You boys build me a big fire in the stove and carry lots of water, and while you're resting, bring in the stuff from the buckboard."

Parker snorted through his nose and stomped out. He went to the barn and saddled his horse. Carrie watched him through the window, but said nothing about it. A moment later Parker rode from the yard and Jethro and Bushrod brought in buckets and mops.

"Ma'am—" Rob Jenner began in protest, then changed his mind when she smiled. "Ma'am, this is right neighborly. Right neighborly indeed."

He grabbed two buckets and went out to the well for water.

As soon as he put the first rise of land between himself and the ranch house, Parker Jenner turned south and rode steadily toward the higher hills. He rode with his head continually swinging, scanning his back trail carefully.

An hour and a half brought him to a timbered rise and he paused, screened by the brush and deep forest shadows. Trixie's cabin was five miles away to the right, completely hidden by smaller peaks that tapered off to the river flats. But below, in the valley where the creek made a quick switchback, Joel McKitrich's house stood in plain view, with the barn and sheds to one side.

Parker studied the lay of the land. A slight spiral of smoke eddied up from the kitchen chimney and he swung his attention to the barn. McKitrich's heavy draught horses were in the corral, along with a pair of harness-broken chestnuts. But his saddle horse was gone.

Parker Jenner left the forest gloom and rode out into the sunlight. He let the horse singlefoot across the yard and when McKitrich's young wife came to the door, Parker swept off his hat. "Mornin'," he said. "I was ridin' past and I thought I'd have a word with Mr. McKitrich."

Shielding her eyes from the sun, Ella McKitrich said, "He ain't here. He went to town an hour ago and won't be back 'til evenin'."

"That's nice," Parker said, and dismounted. He led his horse around the house and tied him, then entered through the back door. Ella McKitrich was bathing the baby in the wash basin and Parker put his arms around her waist and kissed her.

"Don't, Parker," she said, pulling away. "I'm ashamed in front of the baby."

He laughed. "Hell, he can't even talk yet."

"But he can see," Ella said, her full lips compressed. "Parker, I wish you wouldn't come here any more." She dried the baby with a wooly towel and slipped a pair of flannel bloomers on the boy. When she carried him into the bedroom and placed him in the crib, Parker followed her.

When she tried to move past him, he tried to hold her, but she pushed his hands away. "Parker, I mean it. I don't want you to come here no more."

"That ain't so," he said. "You're always waitin' for me, Ella."

"I'm not waitin' no more," she said. "It's—it's wicked, Parker. Downright sinful."

"You don't love him!"

"I guess I don't," she admitted in a soft voice, "but I don't have to be cheatin' either."

He took her arm and pulled her against him, kissing her with a demanding roughness. She struggled against him for a moment, and then her arms whipped around him and she moaned and clung to him.

Parker moved his hands over her back and kissed her cheeks and lips. He bent and scooped her up in his arms. She knew him and tried to stiffen her body, but his grip was strong, his intent determined now.

"No!" she said and pushed at his face. "Parker, the baby. Not in the daylight!"

Laughter bubbled up in him, breaking past his lips. He held her tighter, his mouth brushing hers. He was a man sure of himself, sure of her, and in the end she went limp in his arms, no longer fighting him.

When the baby began to fret, Ella tried to break away

from him, but he held her to him and said, "Let him cry. What the hell?"

"No, Parker," she whispered. "Please, Parker—"

"You talk too much," he said and closed her lips with his own. The baby began to cry in a louder, more demanding voice, but neither of them paid him any attention.

In town, Jim Quartermain stopped before the bank, handed Jane Beal to the ground, then drove to the end of the street and parked the buggy by the stable. Jane and Horace Pendergast were seated in the banker's office when Quartermain came in and took another chair. Pendergast offered him a cigar and a light before saying, "Jane tells me you've already begun to string wire." He puffed energetically on his cigar. "There'll be trouble over that, Quartermain."

"There was trouble over it before," Quartermain said. "This should be no surprise."

"No," Pendergast said, "but as a banker I hate to see it. The whole country will suffer financially. Running W and Long Knife beef have been the major source of revenue in the San Saba. With one gone under and the other weakened—" He spread his hands and let the gesture say the rest.

"Given a little time, shorthorn cattle are going to make you rich," Quartermain pointed out. "Or doesn't that appeal to you?"

"I'm sure Mr. Pendergast is thinking of community prosperity," Jane said, "rather than personal gain."

"Thank you, my dear." The banker beamed. "I was one of Izee Beal's dearest and oldest friends, Jim. Naturally, your involvement in this trouble with the Jenners touches me deeply."

"I've been touched too," Jim Quartermain said, and drew on his cigar. "Touched for several hundred head of steers—I don't know exactly how many."

Pendergast became very attentive and Quartermain added, "The trouble with being a big cattleman is that you never actually know how much you own. The only man who knew was Cimarron when he tallied out at the loading chutes.

"When I went over the books I noticed that the roundup tally and the buyer's tally were alike. Now you know

that just doesn't happen. A roundup tally can be a hundred head off, especially if the crew's in a hurry, and Izee
was. For a while I couldn't figure it, but then it dawned
on me. Cimarron took care of the tally at the loading pens
while Izee and Cherokee went east after Herefords.
Actually, a close tally through the chutes showed several
hundred more steers than Izee or Cherokee thought they
had, so he erased numbers in the tally book and wrote
in the new figures." Quartemain leaned forward in his
chair. "Tell me something, Horace. Did Cimarron de-
posit cash to Running W accounts?"

"Why, yes he did," Pendergast said. "I thought nothing of it at the time." He paused to pull at his lip and dart
a glance at Jane. "My dear, this must be distressing to
you."

"I—it is," she said. "He's been with us so long, it's
hard to think of him as being dishonest."

Quartermain puffed up his cheeks and pushed himself
erect. "Nevertheless I'm going to catch him." He tapped
his cigar against the rim of a glass dish before inserting
it in the corner of his mouth. "How much in cash is Running W worth, Horace?"

"Less than five thousand. Izee invested heavily in the
fence. That costs money, you know. A lot of money."

"I suppose." Quartermain turned to the door. "I'm going down the street. I'm ready to leave any time you are,
Jane."

"Mr. Pendergast and I will talk over old times," she
said sweetly, and gave Quartermain an intimate smile
before he left the bank. The heat of the day was growing
thicker and Pendergast got up and closed the door. The
clerk was waiting on a dumpy woman, his voice running
pleasantly in the manner of men who handle a lot of
money.

Pendergast came back and sat down again. He said,
"Too bad Jim had to find out about Cimarron. If he ever
catches him now—"

"He won't," Jane said. "Cimarron can hide out and
I'll keep Jim Quartermain out of the hills." She smoothed
the folds of her dress and then glanced at Horace Pendergast, who watched her carefully. "I have a hold over Jim
Quartermain that he can't break. In the end he'll dance
the way I want him to."

Pendergast sighed and leaned back in his chair. He put his fingertips together and stared at the pine paneling for a moment. "It was a stroke of genius to finance this venture with Running W money. Let Jim think that Cimarron pocketed the money. The man already has the smell of a thief about him and if Jim should ever catch him and get him to talk, it would be a thief's word against mine. Cimarron made the erasures in the tally book. I didn't. I only cashed the check and kept the difference."

He dropped his cigar in a cuspidor, then fished around in his desk drawer. Withdrawing a packet of letters, he laid them on the blotter and placed his pudgy hand on them. "I detest damning evidence. If you've brought the letters I wrote to you, we can exchange them."

"I brought them," Jane said, and opened her cloth handbag. "I think you'll find they are all there." They exchanged the packets of letters, each one keeping a firm grip on them until their fingers touched the transferring ones. And because there was no trust in them, they examined the contents of each letter until they were satisfied. Pendergast touched a match to his and watched them burn, dropping the ashes in the cuspidor. "Now our bridges are burned, Jane. Nothing can stop us."

"No," she said, "Nothing can. Except Jim Quartermain. I want him for myself, Horace. That was part of the agreement."

He leaned forward in his chair and his manner was fatherly. "And you shall have him. He need never know of this little transaction."

"He'd hate me if he knew," Jane said, and tears formed along her lower eyelids. "He's always understood me, better than Pop or Andy." She raised a hand and brushed at her eyes. "Why did it have to happen to Pop and Andy? Couldn't you have stopped it?"

"There was nothing I could do," Pendergast said simply.

"You lied to me," Jane accused. "Horace, you promised that nothing would happen to Pop and Andy. Licked, yes, but not dead."

Her voice was getting loud and Pendergast grew nervous. He came around the desk and put his arm around her, patting her gently while she cried. "There, there," he said

94

soothingly. "This hit me as hard as it has you. I loved Izee Beal like a brother. That's the gospel truth."

She shook her shoulders and freed herself from his hands. "I've had enough." Her voice was hard. "I want out."

"It's too late," he said. "It was too late two years ago when you came home to visit and we had our little talk, remember? We made an agreement that night, Jane. We both knew that as soon as Izee and Andy got in too deep they'd call Jim Quartermain back, and he had to be controlled. You were going to do that for me, Jane, and because you were, I promised to see that you get half of Rob Jenner's place, plus a clear hand on Running W. You can marry Quartermain for the other half."

She wiped the tears from her eyes and looked at him. "You figured me out well, didn't you? I hate the sight of you."

"Be that as it may," he said, sitting down again, "but love is not a necessary ingredient to the success of my plans. Perhaps I could have found someone in the Jenners—Parker, for instance—who would have gone along with me. Then your Jim Quartermain would *really* have a fight on his hands." He laughed softly. "But we both know the Jenner blood is too thick. They stick together."

"So you picked me."

"Yes," Pendergast said, "and the choice was simple. Izee jokingly complained of your extravagances: dresses, parties. I sensed then that you had developed a taste for money."

"Not enough to see Pop and Andy killed!"

"An unforeseen accident," Pendergast reassured her. "Jane, listen to me now and understand me. Izee and Andy are dead and nothing we can say will change that. But their death is in our favor. Admit it. Now there's only Jim Quartermain left—"

"And he's going to stay alive! I warn you, Horace, if anything happens to Jim I'll blow your schemes so high that—"

"Nothing will happen to him. Jane, we need Jim, we need Jim too much to let anything happen to him."

"And after you no longer need him?"

"My dear, you two will be married and everything will turn out all right." He paused and drummed his fingers on the desk. "Did you know that Quartermain found Trixie?" He saw her puzzlement. "She's a tramp I paid to live in the breaks. She's been acting as go-between for Cimarron and Long Knife. Quartermain gave her a week to clear out and I need her. I can't be running out to Long Knife all the time. Jim damn near caught me the other night."

"Who's this new man at the Jenners? Quartermain knows him."

"Harlow?" Pendergast laughed. "An old friend who once was a partner. But we had a parting of ways. I wired him several times but he had a good thing going in Crystal City. When it blew up, he was more than eager to come here." He stopped quickly, for he had almost added, 'when I told him Quartermain was here.' No use alarming the girl now. "Jane, we need Harlow. The whole deal hinges on the fight between Jenner and Quartermain. When they whittle each other down to pan size, Harlow and his boys can give the Jenners one last punch and it'll be over." He scraped a hand across his lips. "I understand there's a woman at the ranch. Some doctor's daughter from Crystal City."

"She's a sweet thing," Jane said, "and I hate her guts because of it. Right now she's over to Rob Jenner's place baking him pies and being neighborly. Horace, you have to see this girl to appreciate her. She has a way about her that—that wins people."

"Pies?" Pendergast thought about this, his fingers drumming. "This is not at all funny. If I know Rob Jenner, he'll be eating out of her hand inside of an hour. And if he eats out of her hand he's going to visit Quartermain. Jane, we can't have them getting their heads together. Don't you worry about it, though. I'll take care of this personally."

Jane dropped her old letters in her handbag and pulled the drawstring tight. She studied Horace Pendergast and said, "How I regret the day I ever listened to you."

"You're a greedy little thing. You were listening to that."

"Greedy? Horace, when you finish foreclosing on the nesters, you'll own fifteen thousand acres, plus your half of Long Knife. That ought to put you in the neighborhood of thirty thousand acres, hadn't it?"

"Somewhere in that neighborhood," he said and puffed his cigar.

"While I hold half of Running W. That's not much, Horace, and I'm not sure I like it."

"There's your half of Long Knife."

"How can I take that without Jim knowing? You're smart and I'll have to watch you very closely."

"I'll offer it to Quartermain myself," Pendergast said. "When I reap the spoils, he'll understand that I've pulled a fast one. But what can he do except holler a little? He'll take ten thousand and forget it."

"Remember what I said about Jim Quartermain staying alive," Jane said. "He's not going to get it in the back like Bob Lee did."

"I promised you," Pendergast said. "Jane, you'll be the queen of the San Saba."

"And you'll be the king?"

Pendergast chuckled. "Let Jim be the king. I'll be the power behind the thrones. The law will be ours, the judge, the money. Doesn't that appeal to you?"

"I don't know now." She gathered her gloves before moving to the door. There she turned and regarded him again. "Once I thought I could get Jim back by offering him the world. Now I don't think he wants it. Carrie Holderman has what he wants and I'm trying to get it from her so *I* can offer it."

He watched her whisk out onto the street, her long skirts switching. Standing by the window, he pondered this and developed a slight worry.

Maybe she was repenting. Some people did, he realized, although such a thing had never happened to him personally. Pendergast did not like this. He wanted his hirelings to be more rotten than he was and when one of them developed a sudden case of conscience, it disturbed him.

A man shouldn't let his left hand know what his right was doing, he thought. What he promised Jane now did not matter. After the Jenners had been whittled down, Harlow or Audie the Kid could shoot Quartermain in the back and all Jane Beal could do about it would be to cry.

Women were good at that anyway, he decided, and went back to his desk.

CHAPTER 11

After leaving the bank, Jim Quartermain went into the saloon and found Joel McKitrich by the bar, nursing a beer. Quartermain ordered and stood next to McKitrich. McKitrich nodded sagely at the ornate bar, the long mirror, sawdust covered floors and empty poker tables. "Jim," he said, "last time we stood together at a bar like this was in El Paso. We had a gun on each hip and the habit of sizing up every man that walked in."

"Seems like a long time ago," Quartermain said. "I hadn't forgot it though."

"That's the trouble," McKitrich said. "We never really forget. I guess it's because there's nothing real about that kind of life. Always stayin' up all night, prowlin' the streets like a damn animal." He sighed and sipped his beer. "Sometimes I miss it, when I'm honest enough to admit it. Remember that piano player they had in the Texas House in Dodge?" McKitrich smiled faintly. "People don't understand men like us, Jim. They watch us and talk about us, but they don't understand."

"Do we?"

"I guess not," McKitrich said. He finished his beer and slid a quarter on the bar. "On me, Jim. I've got to get back to my place."

"Wait," Quartermain said, and McKitrich turned back. "How is it, Joel? Tough? Giving it up, I mean." He glanced at McKitrich's hips where no gun rested.

"Yeah," the tall man said. "It's not easy. People like to talk and it eats at you."

Quartermain leaned against the bar and swished his beer around in the glass. "You got a wife and son," he said. "I guess that keeps a man going when he gets to thinking, don't it?"

"Yes," McKitrich said. "Yes, it does." McKitrich watched Jim Quartermain, then added, "Can't you make up your mind, Jim?"

"About what?"

"Quittin'. Takin' that gun off and leavin' it off." He chuckled. "I went through the same thing. Always wondered if I could live like any other man who worked for a living. Took me a long time to do it, believe me."

"But what swung you? What happened to make you choose."

"Nothing," McKitrich said. "Absolutely nothing, Jim. I passed through a place on the Trinity nearly five years ago. Fella was livin' there with his family and I had a meal or two with 'em and rode on. A year and a half later I rode through there again and stopped. His place was bigger, the barn finished, he had a new son. Things had changed for him, but not for me. I had on the same boots, pants, hat, even the coat was the same. One of us was movin' and it wasn't me. I guess then was when I made up my mind.

"Had a job waitin' for me, seventy-five a month and twenty per cent of the fines. I never went there, Jim. Turned the horse south and rode until I came to the San Saba. I put my guns in the trunk and haven't taken them out since then."

"You got more guts than I have," Quartermain said. "What about all the trigger-happy kids, Joel? What about them?"

"There haven't been any, Jim. I was a pretty big man, you know. But there hasn't been one solitary man looking for me."

"You're not ramrodding Running W either," Quartermain said.

"Wouldn't want to. Neither do you."

Quartermain looked at his friend oddly. "That doesn't make sense."

"Why don't you fight the Jenners then? That's the way to push them in their hole so you kick in the dirt."

"No," Quartermain said flatly. "There's another way. There *has* to be. A man can't kill every man who disagrees with him."

"Some men do," McKitrich said. "Bickerstaff did."

"I'm not like Bickerstaff!"

"Right now that's a pity," McKitrich said, and signaled the bartender for another beer. "You made a promise to Izee, but he didn't know you any more, Jim. He was remembering the old Quartermain who rode away with Lee

99

of Texas, the Jim Quartermain who *wanted* to pull his gun, the Quartermain that would ride fifty miles to meet a man, the Quart—"

"That's enough!"

"Not too pretty is it?" McKitrich paid for his beer and waited until the bartender walked away. "Jim, that was the way you were. We walked the towns side by side, but we're just ghosts now. Those two men are dead."

Quartermain raised his glass. "Here's to the dead," he said, and finished his beer.

"All you got to do is lay it on the bar and walk away, Jim." McKitrich's voice was gentle. "Just lift it out of the holster and walk away. It's that easy."

"And what do I fight Jenner with? A beer bottle?"

"You said you didn't want to fight him," McKitrich reminded. "Jim, the last couple of years I was travelin', I used to tell myself that I wouldn't meet any man, no matter who he was. But when the time came, I wouldn't back up. I'd wait and they'd come to me and then I'd ride out with the promise shot to hell. But I'd always be ready to make it over again in the next town I hit."

"There's no comparison to this," Quartermain said, and brushed his mustache. "Joel, Rob Jenner says no fence. He means that, and if he makes it stick, Running W is through."

"Maybe it is through," McKitrich said. "Jim, a lot of things are over and done with but men won't let go." He hooked his elbow on the edge of the bar. "The valley's changed. The big augurs are dying out. Jenner's got twenty thousand acres there. Izee had about that but he's cut down to sixteen or thereabouts now. The little men are moving in, Jim. Men like me with a horse and a lot of ambition. You're going to have to do with less and so is Jenner."

"You make him see that?"

"Not me alone, or you alone. But when the time comes and he faces the facts, he's going to back off. Even a fool gets to the point where he can see he won't win."

"But he'll swallow Running W whole and not even belch afterward," Quartermain said.

"Sure," McKitrich agreed. "The squatters will swallow you too but they'll do it so easy you won't know it until you're gone. They're movin' in, Jim. If you and Jenner

100

get into an open fight, they'll pick you clean while you're fighting. Seen that happen in Wyomin'. Couple of the big boys got to squabblin' and while they was shootin' at each other a lot of little men moved in around the edges. The time come to clean 'em all out and neither of the big boys had enough muscle left to do it. The squatters got it all."

Quartermain began to count on his fingers. "There's thirteen families in the San Saba who own less than two sections. That's not many, Joel. Not when Pendergast has been feeding them. A war doesn't help them. It kills them off. Running W and Long Knife is where the money is in the San Saba. When one of us goes to our knees, the whole valley will feel it."

"I won't feel it," McKitrich said. "Pendergast has no note of mine." He looked at his watch. "I'd better be getting back. I've got a way to go."

He went out and Quartermain ordered another beer, toying with it while the minute hand on the wall clock went through a quarter arc. A group of riders stormed into town and flung off in front of the saloon. They spilled onto the porch, shoved the doors aside and stopped, their eyes swinging to Quartermain.

He knew none of them but they were Long Knife riders and the animosity needed no introduction. The bartender came up quickly and took their orders while Quartermain finished his beer.

Through the front window he saw Jane Beal come to the sidewalk and look toward the saloon. Taking this as his cue, he walked out, conscious of the hard stares following him. When he hit the door, one of the riders shot into the ceiling, then laughed when Quartermain started.

He went to the stable then and got the buggy. Pausing by the drygoods store, he got down and helped Jane Beal into the rig. Laughter came from the saloon and he clucked to the team, driving from town.

Jane sensed a purpose behind Quartermain's silence and after they cleared town she said, "What was that shot, Jim?"

"Long Knife inviting me to fight five to one."

She looked at him, not at all sure how to approach him. "I can recall a time when if a man asked for trouble you obliged him."

"That time's passed," Quartermain said, and fell silent again.

As soon as Quartermain's buggy passed the end of the street, Horace Pendergast spoke a few words to the teller, then went out and down the only cross street. His house stood at the edge of town, by a creek shaded with leafy trees. He walked up the path and went inside, directly to the parlor.

Cimarron took his feet off a small table and smiled, a whiskey glass hoisted in salute to gentle living. Pendergast frowned and said, "I have a job for you."

"Easy or hard?"

"Very simple," Pendergast said. "Shoot one of the Jenner boys and see that Jim Quartermain's crew gets blamed for it."

Cimarron forgot the whiskey. He sat up suddenly and said, "Hey, that's pretty risky. What if he shoots me?"

"In the back, you fool!"

"Ah," Cimarron said, again thinking of the whiskey. "I can do that."

"Then get out of here and do it," Pendergast said. "Go over to the Jenner's and tell one of the boys that Trixie has some news. Let him go out by himself, but cut around and wait for him. Make damn sure he's close enough in to the Running W crew so the bushwhacking can be laid on Quartermain's doorstep."

"I will surely do that," Cimarron said, smiling. He went to the hallway, then paused. "Ah, there's a little matter of money, friend."

"Five hundred," Pendergast said.

"When?"

"When I hear about it. Quartermain knows about the beef so you'd better come back here when you're through. You understand?"

"Damn well," Cimarron said, and went out to the barn for his horse.

Out on the flats Joel McKitrich paused when he heard the faint pop of a pistol back in town. McKitrich sat his saddle for several minutes, listening to the great quiet, then rode on toward his own place. Because of the distance from town, the sound of the shot had come seconds late of the actual bullet. A man could be dead before another man heard the shot, he thought, and this struck him as regrettable. He believed a man should die with more purpose than the casual placing of a bullet gave him.

Through the early afternoon McKitrich rode on, sometimes slumped in the saddle, other times riding straight and tall. He pondered Quartermain and the questions he had asked; he recalled asking Cad Pierce that, and Baker, but neither was the kind of man who searched for answers.

McKitrich wondered if a man ever told another the whole truth. He guessed not. Quartermain would believe now that a woman made the difference but McKitrich knew it to be false. Sincerity was a tenuous thing, felt, but rarely pinned down for a man to analyze. He supposed Ella had known why he married her: she was to provide him with an anchor when he recalled too strongly the halcyon days of Joel McKitrich, the two-gun marshal of El Paso and Tascosa. And the pull had been strong, for a man like himself could grow restless without the light of public attention on him.

He came on his place in the late afternoon, rode directly to the barn and off-saddled. He spread out the saddle blanket to dry, rubbed his horse down and grained him, then started across the yard to the house.

In the corral, one of his chestnuts carried a foot lightly and he altered his course to see what was the matter. He spent ten minutes digging a small stone from the hoof, then climbed back through the bars.

Smoke plumed from the kitchen chimney and he could smell the strong flavors of supper. Probably saw me ride across the flats, he thought. Near the back corral gate he noticed horse droppings and paused, genuinely puzzled.

Walking over to the spot, he toed it briefly, then walked slowly toward the back of the house, his head bent. After washing at the low bench beside the door, he went inside and hung up his hat. His wife turned from the stove and gave him a neutral glance.

"You're home early, Joel."

"The town's dead," he said, and sat down at the table, his fingers laced together. "You have a busy day?"

"Like usual." She stirred the fried potatoes over with the spatula. "Hot out on the flats?"

"Like an oven." He said, rolling a cigarette. "You have company?"

She did not turn around. "No." She raised a hand and brushed hair back from her forehead.

His fingers tore the paper of his cigarette and he scooped the mess into his hand and dumped it into the woodbox. He was standing by her now and he said, "I thought maybe one of the others dropped in on you. Been a spell since you've had company."

"There's been no one," she said. "Don't trouble yourself, Joel. I don't mind being alone."

He moved away from her then. The kitchen stifled him. Don't fly off the handle now, he told himself, and stepped outside. The arching sun was making long shadows in the timber a hundred yards in back of the place and he walked up the slope toward the trees.

Moving around, he found the place where the ground was scuffed and the earth littered with droppings. McKitrich leaned against a tree for a moment, his bitterness rising until it almost choked him. Finally he walked back toward the house.

Ella was setting the food on the table. McKitrich took her by the arm. He said, "Who was here this afternoon?"

Her eyes got round and she tried to pull away from his hand. "No one. What's the matter with you?"

"Someone tied a horse in back of the corral," he said evenly. "And someone's been tying a horse in the timber behind the place." He held her eyes now as he had held the eyes of dangerous men, and she became a stranger to him.

"What are you trying to say?" She strained against his grip, but his fingers bit into her arm, stilling her. "Joel! Don't look at me like that!"

"How am I supposed to look? What am I supposed to think, Ella?"

"I don't know what you think!" she yelled. "You're so silent you're like a dummy most of the time!" With her free hand she struck him across the face. He released her and she retreated around the table, keeping it between them.

She began to cry and seemed unaware of it. He watched her, his expression flat and unreadable. "Why, Ella?" he asked. "I've been good to you."

104

"Good?" She mopped at her eyes with the back of hand. "I didn't want to be a housekeeper. That's all you married me for—so you wouldn't have to be alone."

"And why did you marry me?" McKitrich asked. "Because you loved me? Because you couldn't live without me?" He slapped the table hard with the flat of his hand. "We made a bargain, Ella, but you never lived up to your end." He forced the anger out of his voice and out of his eyes. "I want to know, Ella. Who is he?"

"I ain't going to tell you," she said. "I'll take the baby and go if you want, but I ain't going to tell."

"The boy stays," McKitrich said. "I don't care what you do or where you go, but he don't go with you."

"No!" she said. "Joel, don't do this to me!"

"You done it to yourself," he told her. "I want his name, Ella. I mean to get it too."

She saw no give in his face and knew that he would never bend in his demand. For a time she remained stubbornly silent. Then she asked, "What are you going to do, Joel?"

"Kill a man," he said without feeling.

She shook her head. "Don't do that. It ain't that I love him, Joel. It was just that I was so lost."

"We're all lost," McKitrich said. "Speak his name, Ella."

She bent her head forward and her voice was a little more than a whisper. "Parker Jenner."

"Thank you," he said, and went into the bedroom. When he came out a moment later, he was buckling on his gunbelt and a holstered pistol sat well forward on each hip. He thumbed cartridges from the loops, cartridges green with verdigris. McKitrich wiped them on a towel and loaded both guns. His wife watched him without emotion.

Finally she said, "You wanted a home and no more guns and now I've taken that away from you. Joel, don't do this on account of me."

"There's no choice," he said, and a wry, fatalistic smile lifted one corner of his lips. "I was a fool to ever think there'd be a stopping once a man set his feet in that direction."

He took his hat and tugged it low on his forehead. Pausing in the door he said, "Don't have any overpowerin' regrets, Ella. We are what we are and there ain't no way we can change it."

"I'm so ashamed, Joel. Do you believe that?"

"I guess I do," he said, and went out for his horse.

The sun was well down now and a grayness was invading the land. He rode away from his place, not once looking back, and for better than an hour he stayed near the edge of the flats.

To his left, a ragged line of hogbacks cut him off from Quartermain's Running W, and on impulse, McKitrich turned the horse and began to climb. For three miles he rode on until darkness found him dropping off on the other side.

A trail ran through here, leading to Trixie's isolated place miles beyond. McKitrich stopped and rolled a smoke while he listened to the silence around him. He was finishing his smoke when he heard a sound. His attention sharpened. Ahead of him along the path, a horse's hoof plopped in the dust. He stood in the stirrups, trying to make out the rider, but too much distance lay between them.

Without hurry, McKitrich moved ahead at a slow walk, his cigarette pinched out now. A rocky uplift bracketed him on his left, and on the right, stunted timber made the night black. Suddenly a gun blasted and woke echoes through the hills, and from the muzzle flash McKitrich judged it to be no more than seventy yards ahead.

He drove his heels to his horse and came up quickly. One man was down in the trail and McKitrich's horse shied at the smell of blood. McKitrich found another man there also, a surprised man. He threw a shot at McKitrich and wheeled to run.

There was some light and McKitrich had closed up to ten yards. He saw the man whirl to snap a shot. Then the fellow changed his mind and dashed away at a mad run. McKitrich did not pursue, but dismounted by the man in the path.

He scratched a match and recognized Forney Jenner. The man had been 'dusted from both sides,' the bullet having passed clean through him, taking out a section of the right breast and lung. From the blood on Forney's lips and the wildly rolling eyes, McKitrich knew that he had only seconds left.

"Who did it? Forney, can you hear me?"

"Cim—ron," Forney gasped and died. The match burned Joel McKitrich's fingers and he dropped it. He got up and moved down the path to where Forney's horse patiently waited.

CHAPTER 12

Jim Quartermain was in a savage mood when he returned to the ranch with Jane Beal, and she knew him well enough to remain silent. The bitter thought that he had been forced to waste a man's life rankled in his mind, and beneath this lay the shattering news that Jane had dropped earlier in the day.

Carrie Holderman had not returned by dark and Quartermain went out to the front porch with his thoughts and cigar. Cherokee came across the yard, intent on conversation, but soon gave it up and went back.

Purvis tried an hour later, but made no headway. He smoked a cigar in silence, then stretched and went back to the bunkhouse. Near ten, the sound of laughter and Rob Jenner's rough voice overrode the rattle of the buckboard and a moment later the cavalcade pulled into the yard.

Jethro jumped down from his horse, handed Carrie out of the rig and brought her onto the porch. Rob Jenner saw Quartermain in the shadows and said, "Man, I had no hand in that the other night."

Jenner was smoking a cigar and he gave Carrie an affectionate grin. "This is some little woman, Quartermain, dadblamed if she ain't. Curried the place proper, then baked me'n my son a pie."

"Where's Parker and Forney?" Quartermain asked.

"Skylarkin'," Rob said. "Parker's been gone all day. Forney left this afternoon." He wiped his huge hands on his legs and said, "Seems a damn shame we got to have this quarrel between us. I mean, hell—it ain't neighborly at all. It surely ain't."

Cherokee, expecting trouble, came across the yard at

107

a run, but Jim Quartermain waved him back. "You want to come in, Rob?" Quartermain asked. Carrie Holderman leaned against the porch railing, watching these men reach out to each other, testing the bare seeds of understanding.

"Oh, I guess not tonight," Rob Jenner said. "It's late and we ought to be startin' back." He glanced at Carrie. "You're welcome any time, ma'am. I mean that now."

"I'm sure you do, Mr. Jenner," Carrie said, looking around as Jane Beal came to the doorway.

"Maybe we can get together for some talk," Jenner said to Jim Quartermain. "Likely as not this thing can be settled without a lot of bleedin' on both sides."

"That's been my thought all along," Quartermain said, and walked with the Jenners to their horses. Rob and Jethro swung heavily to the saddles and along the edge of the yard a man spoke sharply, drawing everyone's attention.

The bunkhouse door opened and light flooded in a puddle. Purvis came out and joined Cherokee, who was talking to the shadowy rider. They came on in a group, and in the light coming from the front door, Joel McKitrich dismounted. On the horse behind him, Forney Jenner lay head down.

Rob Jenner cursed and swung from his horse. He lifted Forney's head, then dropped it back against the saddle skirt. He faced McKitrich. "Did you do this, man? In the back!"

"No," McKitrich said with such quiet conviction that no man there doubted him. He looked at Quartermain and there was an apology in his eyes. "Cimarron did it. Jim. I'm sorry, but he did."

Rob Jenner's swearing was a monument to his flaring anger. He turned to Quartermain and said, "I see this now in a different light. While she charms me with her honey words and fancy cookin' my son's shot in the back by Running W!" He shook his fist in Quartermain's face. "Damn you and this brand! You want war, you'll get war now!"

He swung to Jethro. "Mount up!" They went into the saddles again. "Mark me now, Quartermain—there'll be no let-up! Not until you're dead and your cattle scattered and your buildings burned to the ground!"

Jerking their horses around, the Jenners stormed from the yard at a gallop. Quartermain stood there and watched them leave, powerless to do anything about it.

Purvis and Cherokee walked back to the bunkhouse. Jim Quartermain said, "Come in, Joel." He took Carrie's arm, brushed past Jane and went into the parlor.

There he noticed that McKitrich wore his revolvers. He said nothing, but a large question formed in his eyes. Carrie's face was bleak as she sat on the sofa. Jane leaned against the arch and looked from one to the other.

"What happened out there?" Quartermain asked.

McKitrich recounted his movements from the time he left his place until he rode into Quartermain's yard. "I went to Long Knife first," he said. "That Harlow fella said the Jenners were here, bringing her home." He nodded to Carrie Holderman. "I'm sorry, Jim, but Forney said Cimarron's name just before he died. There was another man there, all right, 'cause he took a shot at me and then lit out."

Quartermain stripped the wrapper off a cigar, taking his light from the lamp chimney. "You don't have to answer this, Joel, but what were you doing out?" He nodded at the guns. "What made you change your mind?"

"Personal score to settle," McKitrich said dryly, and from his manner Quartermain knew that he would say no more.

Jane left her place in the archway and came into the room to sit down. She said, "Carrie, I don't want to blame you but you should have listened to me. I know the Jenners and they're unpredictable as bears. Can't you see what you've done?"

"No," Carrie said. "Since when has it been wrong to be nice to someone?"

"What Jane's trying to say," Quartermain explained, "is that if you hadn't gone over there, Rob Jenner wouldn't feel so bitter about this. Your being there made it look like a plan, a deliberate trick on our part to get Rob off guard so Forney could be killed."

"But it wasn't!" Carrie said hotly, glancing from Quartermain to Jane and back.

"Carrie," Jane said patiently, "I'm leaning backward, but I can't go on leaning. You had no right to go over there. Jim didn't want you to and I asked you not to,

109

but you went anyway. If you insist on staying here any longer—and I see no reason why you should—please don't interfere with ranch business."

Quartermain saw that Carrie Holderman was near tears. He looked at McKitrich and found him regarding this impersonally. Quartermain said, "If we had trouble before this, it's nothing to what we're going to have. Up to now I had hoped that somehow we could get together, Rob and me, and talk this thing out." He shook his head. "That's gone now. He'll oil up his gun and come back." Raising his eyes to McKitrich, he asked, "You think Rob would listen if I found Cimarron and made him talk?"

"No," McKitrich said. "Cimarron'll be hard to locate, Jim, and you haven't much time. Rob'll bury his boy tomorrow. Better be ready for him after that because he'll be here."

"I know it." Quartermain bit the end off a cigar. "Which way was Cimarron heading? Toward the breaks?"

McKitrich shook his head. "Toward Trixie's place. You figure it out. I can't."

"Sure," Quartermain said slowly. "That adds up."

Jane, who was watching Jim Quartermain carefully, said, "Don't do anything foolish now, Jim. Cimarron is a dangerous man on the run. He wouldnt' hesitate to kill you."

"I might not hesitate when it comes to killing him either," Jim Quartermain said. He turned to McKitrich. "Go tell Purvis and Cherokee I want them." McKitrich went out, his boots rattling across the porch. Jim Quartermain puffed on his cigar until his head and shoulders were wreathed in smoke.

Within Jane Beal's mind, a worry began as a fester and grew. She knew Jim Quartermain and how he was when he locked his mind on something, and now he was determined to find Cimarron, a thing she did not want. For the hundredth time she cursed the day she had first listened to Horace Pendergast, but it was too late now for regrets. She had no way of knowing how much Pendergast had told Cimarron. If the lanky Texan knew about her and told Jim Quartermain . . . The risk was too great.

"Jim," she said, "don't go. I have a feeling."

"A feeling about what?"

"Just a feeling," she said. "There's going to be a fight and I don't want you away when it happens."

"I'll be back," he said, and went back to his thoughts.

Jane looked at Carrie Holderman and found the girl watching her steadily. Taking a deep breath, Jane said, "I've tried to be nice to you, Carrie, even when I didn't want to be."

"That was sweet of you," Carrie said sarcastically. "I'm sure that must have cost you."

"I'm not looking for a fight now," Jane said evenly, holding her temper in check. "If you have any influence on Jim Quartermain, then use it now. Do it for him, not for me."

"Why should I?" Carrie said. She looked at Jim Quartermain. "Do I have any influence over you?"

"No," he said bluntly. "Carrie, right now I wish you'd never come here. All of a sudden I think Jane's right. You don't belong here. I'm sorry, Carrie, but you always liked honest answers."

The girl bit her lip and clasped her hands tightly together. "That's being frank, isn't it?" She got up quickly and went out to the porch.

McKitrich came back in then with Cherokee and Gil Purvis at his heels. "What you got in mind?" Cherokee asked.

"I'm going after Cimarron," Quartermain said. "Can I count on you, Joel?"

McKitrich nodded. "I'm lookin' for a man and until I find him, you can."

"That's good enough for me," Quartermain said. "Gil, have one of the boys saddle me a good horse. Cookie can make up a sack. I want two blankets, a rifle, a slicker and I guess that's all. You equipped for a long ride, Joel?"

"I'll get by," McKitrich said, and twirled a smoke.

"Gil, after we leave, go out to the fence and tell the boys to stay wide awake. Have them dig some shallow trenches on this side of the fence and move into them. When Jenner rides, he's going to have Harlow and his toughs with him and the boys will need cover. Tell them to put up as stiff a fight as they can, then run for the ranch when it gets too hot."

"I'll do that," Purvis said. "All right if I stay out there with 'em?"

"Sure," Quartermain said, and Purvis went outside. McKitrich still leaned against the wall with his cigarette. Jane sat on the arm of a chair, worried and trying not to show it.

Quartermain spoke to Cherokee. "Put two outriders around the place here. I doubt Rob will be back tonight, but he'll be back. McKitrich says Cimarron was heading for Trixie's place. Right now it doesn't make sense, but I'm going after him. Likely I'll be back sometime tomorrow. Allow no one to come and go. Just keep the men around the place and see that everyone is armed with a rifle."

"I'll take care of it." Cherokee stomped out. McKitrich finished his cigarette and went outside.

Jane continued to watch Jim Quartermain. Finally she said, "What you said to her, Jim—did you mean that?"

"I said it, didn't I?"

"But did you mean it? There's never been a second best with me, Jim. I want to know."

"We'll talk about it when I get back," he said, and threw his cigar in the fireplace.

Jane smiled. "Now you're the Jim I remember. You're the king, Jim. You were born to rule."

From outside Purvis yelled, "Jim! McKitrich's waitin'!"

"All right, I'm coming!" He picked up his hat and stepped outside. Carrie was on the porch. On impulse he walked over to her and said, "Can I say I'm sorry?"

"You've said it, but I don't think you are," she said. "You finally got it said, didn't you? I've been wondering when you would."

"I didn't want to say it," he told her, "but you have a way of pushing at a man."

"Come out with it and clear it off your chest," Carrie invited. The lamplight touched her face and her eyes were moist, but she held her head erect and met him squarely.

"Maybe I better," he said. "Maybe I was flattered in Crystal City when you played it just fast enough to be interesting. I liked it. I see now that I *was* displeased when you came here. You don't belong, Carrie. You're city and you just don't fit. There are no back yard fences to chat over. You better go home. That's the best thing."

"I will go home now!" she snapped, and tears spilled down her cheeks. "Go on, King! When you come back I

112

won't be here!" She pushed past him and rushed into the house.

From the yard, McKitrich said softly, "If we're goin', let's go."

Quartermain went off the porch and mounted. They trotted from the yard and Quartermain traveled for an hour toward the distant hills, passing the fence by a wide margin. When the land steepened he dismounted to lead and Joel McKitrich followed.

After midnight, Quartermain stopped at a trickle of water coming from the rocks and drank. McKitrich squatted beside him, drank deeply, then said, "The world can go to hell fast for a man, can't it?"

Quartermain tried to cut the darkness and read McKitrich's face. "You're back where you started, Joel. I guess we both are."

"Where we belong," McKitrich said. "A man's a fool to think he can wipe out the past just by sayin' it never happened." He shook out his sack of tobacco, fashioned a cigarette, then threw the empty sack away. After he got a match to it, he said, "I was never much for givin' a man advice, Jim, but I'm goin' to pass on some now. There was a girl in El Paso. Likely you don't remember her, but she wasn't much. Neither was I. We should have got married, Jim. We'd have lived high for a year or two. Then someone would have got me and she'd have gone her way with someone else just like me." His cigarette glowed a moment. "But I didn't want that. Had to get me a quiet woman and make my peace with myself. Only there wasn't no peace.

"Seems that you're tryin' to do the same with the young filly on the porch. Don't marry her if you don't love her, Jim. It don't work out."

Because they were old friends, Quartermain listened without offense. And because they were both deeply troubled men of the gunsmoke brotherhood, Quartermain could ask, "Family troubles, Joel?"

"Busted up," McKitrich admitted. "That happens." He sighed and drew deeply on his smoke. "I wanted to quit, Jim. Just to stay alive. That's why I married her, to drop away from the places I'd been, the people I knew. I married her to put up my pistols and now I find that I'm takin' 'em up again. You figure it out. I can't."

Quartermain stood up and stamped his legs, then mounted. McKitrich stubbed his cigarette and moved out when Quartermain did. They followed a ridge for three miles, then cut across a shallow valley and over another rise. Around one-thirty Quartermain paused and looked down at the solitary cabin that was Trixie's home. McKitrich said, "Here?"

"He goes here," Quartermain said. "If he's not here, we'll wait."

"Why not?" McKitrich said. "I got lots of time." Saddle leather creaked as he shifted his weight. "I want Parker, Jim."

"All right," Quartermain said, and remained silent because he had no more need for talk. The story was clear to him now and he regretted deeply that McKitrich's dream should be so abruptly shattered. He had known many gunfighters. They all talked about a place of their own, or a woman, but few ever realized their dreams. Quartermain supposed that Joel McKitrich had, for a short time, known peace. But the woman who offered this to him took it away without knowing what she was doing. She lifted him from his dangerous existence and then returned him to it.

"Better dismount and walk," Quartermain said, and they picketed the horses on the hillside, screened by brush.

They saw a light burning inside the cabin as they approached. Pausing by the door, Quartermain heard slight sounds of movement, then lifted the latch carefully and drove the panel open with his shoulder.

Trixie shrieked. Cimarron made a dive for his gun, but Quartermain lifted the muzzle of his rifle and said, "Forget it." Joel McKitrich stepped inside and toed the door closed. He looked around the bare room and then stared at Cimarron who stood in the middle of the floor.

"Get your breeches on," Quartermain said, and scooped them off the table, tossing them to Cimarron. Next, he removed the cartridges from Cimarron's gun and threw them in the wood box.

Trixie sat up on the edge of the bed and McKitrich said, "That's good enough. Behave yourself now."

Cimarron fastened his belt and glared at Quartermain. "What the hell's the big idea? Who stepped on your corn anyway?"

114

"We're going to pay off now," Quartermain said. "For the beef you sold, and the money you kept, and Forney Parker's killing."

"Ha," Cimarron said. "You can go to hell, Quartermain. There's no way you can prove anything on me. I'm clean as hell." He swung his head to Trixie. "Tell him how long I been here, honey."

"Since sundown," she said.

"You're a liar," Quartermain told them. "Both of you."

"I'm the guy you took a shot at," McKitrich said quietly, and watched the shock appear on Cimarron's face.

Cimarron licked his lips. He appealed to Jim Quartermain. "You wouldn't shoot a man without hearin' his side, would you?"

"No," Quartermain said. "I'd shoot him afterward."

Cimarron's eyes flicked from Quartermain to McKitrich. "Can I sit down?" When neither man answered, he spread his hands in an appealing gesture. "Forney pulled on me, Jim. You don't know this, but I've been spyin' on Long Knife and Forney got wind of it somehow. He wanted me to take a ride with him, show me somethin'. Then the devil whipped out his pistol. I shot in self-defense."

"In the back," McKitrich said. "Sure, I believe you, Cimarron. I carted the body home to the old man."

Quartermain backed up until he touched the table, then sat on one corner, his rifle still covering Cimarron. "You're about the biggest liar I ever saw, Cimarron. First, you made a few changes in the books and pocketed the money that belonged to Running W. Then you up and shot Forney in the back. This all your idea, Cimarron?"

"Maybe," the man said guardedly. "What difference would it make? You're going to kill me anyway."

"That may be true," Quartermain said, "but the truth would make a difference how—easy or hard as hell." He took a cigar from his pocket, nipped off the end, then cracked a match on his thumbnail. "You're a stupid man, Cimarron. You always were. So naturally I can't give you the credit for thinking up all these cute stunts. Who gives the orders?"

"Nobody."

Quartermain spoke to McKitrich without turning his head. "There's an uncured hide hanging in the lean-to.

115

Bring me in a good-sized strip of it. Then start carrying in firewood."

McKitrich went out. Cimarron watched Quartermain, growing increasingly nervous as time passed. Finally McKitrich came back and laid a strip of stiffened hide on the table. Quartermain edged toward the stove, took the lid off the teakettle, and forced the rawhide into the water until it grew as soft as cloth.

"Build up that fire," Quartermain said. "Get it hot as hell in here, Joel." McKitrich started to chuck wood into the stove and Quartermain kicked a chair toward Cimarron. He tied the man's hands to the chair, then cut another strip of rawhide two feet long and an inch wide. This he wound around Cimarron's head, just above the eyebrows. McKitrich had the fire roaring and Quartermain went back to the table to sit.

"The Apaches use this to make a man talk," Quartermain said. "The heat will begin to shrink the rawhide in an hour or two and I understand that it'll pop a man's eyes right out of his head."

From the bed, Trixie began to whimper. McKitrich silenced her with a sharp glance. Cimarron began to fight the bonds around his wrists and sweat popped out on his forehead and ran down his face.

No one spoke and the heat in the small room began to build until perspiration was damp on them all. Cimarron's breathing was loud and ragged and Quartermain watched the man, his face inscrutable.

CHAPTER 13

The stove top glowed a dull red and McKitrich's shirt was spotty with sweat. Trixie sat like a woman enchanted, her only movement an occasional twitch in her face. Still sitting on the corner of the table, Quartermain waited and watched while Cimarron's breathing sawed loudly in the room.

The rawhide was tightening slowly, steadily. Occasionally it popped gently and Cimarron's eyes grew more wild and terror stricken. He was in pain, Quartermain knew; but not enough pain, for he refused to speak.

An hour passed, then two. McKitrich peered out the window once and said, "Be daylight soon."

"We got lots of time," Quartermain said.

"I can't stand this," Trixie said, near tears. "Are you human?"

"Usually," Quartermain said, "but this is one of my off days."

He continued to wait. Suddenly Cimarron's scream blasted the quiet: *I can't stand it! Take it off!*

"You ready to tell the truth?" Quartermain asked.

Cimarron nodded and Quartermain opened the blade of his jack knife, cutting the binding and dropping it to the floor. With the sudden release of pressure, Cimarron's head fell forward and he sat that way for several minutes.

"Better start," Quartermain said. "I won't wait."

McKitrich opened the front door and kicked the glass out of the one window.

"Hey," Trixie said, "this is my house."

"You're leaving," Quartermain told her, and focused his attention on Cimarron. "What made you feel so damn immune that you'd come here after murdering Forney Jenner?"

The cool night wind coming in through the open door and window seemed to revive Cimarron. He raised his head and asked, "You let me go if I tell you?"

"No," Quartermain said. "I'll just see that you get hung legal." He let Cimarron consider this for a moment, then added, "We can use some more rawhide, but this time I'll put it on, board up the place and leave you here."

"I'll tell you," Cimarron said. "I'm just a flunky, same as Trixie is."

"Flunky for who?"

"Pendergast," Cimarron said. "He wants you to fight the Jenners, so he can foreclose on the squatters. I was in town when you were. He told me to take Forney out for a gallop, but to come back alone."

"And to be sure and do it on Running W land, was that it?"

"Yeah."

"Who got the money for the Running W beef you made off with?"

"Pendergast," Cimarron said. "I got two hundred. He got the rest. It's payin' the salary of Harlow and the toughs." He raised his eyes to Quartermain's. "You go ahead and see me hung, but I won't hang. I'm goin' to get off, you wait and see. Pendergast has got you where the hair is short and he's pullin' hard. You think the Jenners are goin' to listen to talk after what happened to Forney? They wouldn't even believe me if I told 'em Pendergast paid me to do it."

"We're going to find that out," Quartermain said, and hustled Cimarron outside. Trixie followed with McKitrich right behind them. The first light of dawn was rinsing the sky and the outline of the timber became more clear as the minutes filed past. "Get Cimarron's horse," Quartermain said, "then go in and dump over that stove."

"The place'll burn!" Trixie shrieked.

"That's possibly true," Quartermain said.

McKitrich came back a moment later with Cimarron's mount, then went up the hill after their own horses. When he returned, the daylight was stronger and he went inside the cabin. The stovepipe came down with a crash, and the stove followed a moment later.

By the time he got to the door, the flames were already licking up the walls. Trixie began to cry. Cimarron mounted at Quartermain's invitation, then McKitrich touched Quartermain on the arm and pointed to a rise above the timber.

Parker Jenner sat his horse there, not more than five hundred yards away. Trixie saw him and laughed. "He's been to your place, McKitrich. Layin' up with your wife."

McKitrich did not glance at her, but his jaws tightened. He waited, his eyes never leaving Parker Jenner. Finally he spoke to Quartermain. "This is as far as I go, Jim."

Parker recognized McKitrich and came off the slope at a walk. He dismounted when he was thirty yards away, and led his horse. He looked at the cabin, now breaking out with fire, and at Cimarron who sat his horse, still under Quartermain's gun.

But his eyes lingered longest on Joel McKitrich. Parker said, "I guess it's out of the bag now, ain't it?"

"Yes," McKitrich said. "You going to marry her?"

"I guess not," Parker said, smiling slightly. "But she was fun, I'll say that much."

Color drained from McKitrich's face. "Parker, you're pretty calm for a man who's going to die."

"I'm not dead yet," Parker said. He flipped his eyes to Quartermain. "Where do you fit in this?"

"He doesn't," McKitrich said. "This is between you and me, Parker. No matter how this turns out, Jim, it's all right. Do I have your word on it?"

"You have my word," Quartermain said, and he stood where he could cover Cimarron and Trixie and watch the other two at the same time.

Parker laughed and said, "I've heard a lot about you and the old days, McKitrich. Been times when I've wondered if it was all a lot of brag."

"You'll find out," McKitrich said. "I'll wait for you, Parker."

"Just like a duel, eh?" Parker's smile deepened. "I heard about that too, some crazy honor code you gunfighters had. Personally, I never thought much of it."

His right hand whipped up and across his body and his gun came clear as McKitrich drew. Parker cocked as the gun came around, matching Joel McKitrich's movement. Then the gun in Parker's hand blasted and McKitrich stumbled, triggering his shot into the ground by Parker's feet.

Cimarron took his chance then. He kicked at the barrel of the rifle in Quartermain's hands. The shot ripped through the trees on the hillside, and then Cimarron was bending low on the horse's neck and racing down the valley. Forgetting everything but his man, Quartermain worked the action and fired once at a distance of seventy-five yards. Cimarron made a slow roll as he left the horse, and then he lay in the grass where the bullet had tagged him, sick and helpless with a shattered shoulder.

From the edge of his vision, Quartermain caught Parker Jenner's movement. He whirled, but Parker was just mounting his horse. Trixie ran to him, and he edged his horse away from her and fended her off with his foot, all the time watching Quartermain.

"That's one less gunfighter," Parker said. "He wasn't as good as he thought, was he?" He laughed and wheeled

119

his horse. "I want to get *you* in town where people can see it and talk about it."

He dashed away then and behind the cabin and the flaming wall gave way in a shower of sparks. Quartermain put his rifle down and lifted McKitrich's shoulders. The man was bleeding badly from the mouth and a large stain was spreading over his stomach.

"Got me where it hurts," McKitrich said between ragged breaths. "Don't end up like this, Jim." He coughed and a rattling began in his throat. Trixie watched with wide eyes as McKitrich's life left him with a rush. The ridge pole burned through, allowing the roof to collapse, and the heat began to mount steadily. Quartermain lifted McKitrich and put him on his horse, then gathered his rifle and the reins of his own.

"You're not going to leave me here?" Trixie asked.

"Take Cimarron's horse," he said. "Help him on it and ride double. Go in to Pendergast and tell him I sent you. He hired both of you so let him worry about you. Tell Pendergast I didn't have to kill Cimarron. Tell him I'll be in to see him soon."

He led McKitrich's horse out of the clearing. On the highest ridge he looked back, watched the cabin burn for a moment, then went on.

Because he walked the horses, he did not raise McKitrich's cabin until eight. McKitrich's wife saw Quartermain approaching and came to the door. When she recognized her husband draped across the saddle, she began to run. Quartermain dismounted stiffly and looked at her. She did not go near Joel McKitrich and tears made bright streaks down her cheeks.

"Parker Jenner did this," Quartermain said, "if it gives you any satisfaction to know."

"You hate me, don't you?"

"No," Quartermain said, "but I feel sorry for you." He wanted to tell her about Joel McKitrich and the old days, but there were no words in him to make her see. She had not lived in the bad towns and walked the streets every night with danger like a current around her. She would never understand how precious the dream of peace could be.

"I couldn't touch him," she said softly. "Could you—"

Quartermain shook his head. He wanted to do this final

120

thing for his friend, but he was human and wanted to hurt her. He said, "He's your man. He gave you his name even though you didn't think enough of him to honor it."

He turned to his horse and mounted. "Mrs. McKitrich, he met Parker fair and straight out. But he was a fool. He loved you enough to die for your honor."

"You do hate me," she said, and watched Quartermain ride from the yard and down the narrow valley foot.

Memories paraded Indian file through Quartermain's mind, memories of Dodge and the Long Branch. He and McKitrich walking the streets together, to be watched, to be talked about: "He killed that fellow from Montana last fall in Abilene." . . . "Was you in El Paso when they packed the law on the hip?" . . . "And then Bass came out of the Occidental and crossed the street. Four men behind him, but there they stood. Bass left town in ten minutes. . . ."

Those were the portions of a man's life that he remembered, Quartermain decided. Those moments when he stood ready to deliver, to fight and perhaps to die. All other moments were just time, and a man ate and slept and acted like any other man.

But we're not like other men, he told himself. We'll never be like them again. People recognize us and expect us to have four hands.

He shook his head gently and rode on.

Noon was approaching when he rode into his own yard and slipped off the horse. Cherokee Nye came from the barn as Quartermain went into the house. He stopped in the hallway, for Jane and Carrie were there and Carrie had been crying.

Beneath a blanket, a man lay on the horsehair sofa. Quartermain turned as Cherokee came in. "Purvis," Cherokee said. "The Jenner boys caught him early this morning and dumped him in our yard. They hung him."

Quartermain peeled the blanket away from Purvis' face. He grimaced and pulled the blanket up again.

"Gil went out to check the fence crew," Carrie said. "Jim, did they have to do this?"

"I don't know," he said. He sat down and cradled his head in his hands, weariness rounding his shoulders. "Cimarron's gone. I caught him at Trixie's place. He tried running, but I winged him in the shoulder then sent him

121

off with Trixie. McKitrich is dead. Parker Jenner came along while we were at Trixie's and they got in a fight."

"What does that matter now?" Jane asked. She still wore her robe and bedroom slippers. "Jim, gather the crew and we'll ride on Long Knife. We can't stand still and take this."

"Let's come off the boil," Quartermain said. He remained silent for a while, then said, "Gil was my friend, the only friend I had when I needed one bad, but I can't hate the Jenners for this. Cimarron killed Forney and now they're paying us back. But then, Cimarron only pulled the trigger on Forney. Horace Pendergast is the man who's going to pay for it."

Carrie raised her head. Cherokee paused with the manufacturing of a cigarette. A quick caution appeared in Jane Beal's eyes and she said, "What do you mean, Jim?"

"I caught Cimarron and made him talk," Quartermain said. He began to recount the man's story and Jane Beal listened with increased nervousness.

She kept her face smooth and unreadable, even while her mind raced for answers that would satisfy Jim Quartermain. Her fear that Cimarron knew of her part in Pendergast's schemes had been groundless. Quartermain did not suspect her. But she had to keep him from suspecting.

"Jim," she said, "has it ever occured to you that Cimarron was lying to you?"

"Yes," he admitted, "but I think he was telling the truth. He implicated Trixie in this whole mess and she made no denial of it. I believe he was talking straight."

Jane rubbed her hands together and blew out a disgusted breath. "But the whole thing is so far fetched, Jim. How did Pendergast know that Cimarron was going to handle the shipping at the railhead? And he must have if—as you say—Cimarron sold the stock to finance Pendergast. Jim, you know Horace has tried to prevent a fight between Running W and Long Knife. He's doomed to failure unless he—"

"Unless he what?" Quartermain asked quietly.

"I was going to say, unless he had help from Running W or Long Knife." She laughed. "At first thought that seems ridiculous, but on second glance it isn't. I thought of Parker Jenner, how wild he is now. Why couldn't he be working with Pendergast? After all, Cimarron could have made his brag to Trixie about being shipping boss. Then suppose she passed it to Parker and he passed it to Pendergast. It's obvious that someone passed it on from her, because Horace would never go there. I'm saying all this on the assumption that Cimarron *could* have been telling the truth. Personally, I think it's a lie to save his own neck."

Quartermain sat hunched forward in his chair, mulling it over. Jane leaned against the wall, her eyes veiled.

She was sure that she could not stop Quartermain from talking to Pendergast, but in planting the seed of Parker Jenner in his mind, she could channel his thinking and cover her own tracks.

Carrie Holderman had been watching Jane. Now she got up and left the room. Quartermain did not appear to notice her. In her own room she heard Quartermain's voice; then she closed the door and slipped out of her dress. She dropped her petticoats and stripped off her shirtwaist. She remembered the window and drew the curtains together. She slipped into a pair of blue jeans. The denim felt cold and stiff against her legs. She put on a flannel shirt, tucking it in as she went out and through the kitchen. At the barn she had one of the men saddle a horse for her, then mounted and walked him from the yard. She heard the bunkhouse door slam and Cherokee's yell floated out, but she did not turn around to look at him.

The sun promised to be hot and already heat was driving through the weave of her shirt. In her mind she tried to validate her actions and could not. She sensed a false note in Jane's theory and could not put her finger on it. This bothered her, for she was a girl who liked to have a reason to substantiate her foolishness.

"And this *is* foolishness," she said out loud to herself.

During the night her hurt had diminished and she had changed her mind about leaving, at the same time wondering how she would tell Jim Quartermain of this change. Some force within her just would not let her leave the field to Jane Beal. With a woman's intuition she believed that Jane was not honest, either with Quartermain or herself.

Now that she had heard Quartermain's account of Cimarron's confession and heard Jane Beal poo-poo the

whole thing, Carrie was convinced that she understood
Jim Quartermain well enough to know that he would hold
Rob Jenner responsible for Gil Purvis' hanging.

And they'll start shooting, Carrie thought.

At the fence, she waved to the crew and lifted the horse
into a trot. An hour later she cut across the land toward
Long Knife. She rode boldly into the yard and slipped off
the horse by the porch. Rob Jenner came out, his face
like thunder.

"You're not welcome on this land, woman!"

Carrie walked up the steps and faced him. "Do you consider yourself a fair man?"

"Yes," Jenner said. "But I'll have no more truck with
Running W."

"Then if you're fair, you'll listen," Carrie said. "Can I
come in?"

"No," Jenner said flatly. "Speak your piece and then go.
But don't come back."

"All right." Carrie hoisted herself on the porch rail.
"Mr. Jenner, are you sure that Quartermain is out to ruin
you?"

"Yes," Jenner said. "His man killed my boy, Forney."

"And this morning, Quartermain shot Cimarron for
it," Carrie said, watching the disbelief on Rob Jenner's
face. "Send a man to Trixie's place and see for yourself."

"To run into a trap?"

"I'll go with you, if I have to," Carrie said. "Mr. Jenner,
let's both assume that Jim Quartermain didn't have anything to do with Forney's death."

"But he did," Jenner said flatly.

"Let's pretend he didn't. Let's say that Cimarron was
working for Pendergast—" Carrie watched his face carefully— "just like Harlow and the others are."

Jenner stared at her and his manner became guarded.
"All right. I'll pretend."

Carrie began to touch off the points on her fingers.
"Pendergast has money tied up and holds mortgages that
he'll foreclose, providing he can stir up the country. To
do that, he has to see that you and Quartermain fight. And
when you get together to make peace, as you were ready
to do the other night, he has to do something about it."

"But how did he know about that in time?" Jenner said,
sure that he had caught Carrie.

124

"While we're pretending," Carrie said, "let's pretend that either one of your sons or someone on Running W is working with Pendergast. Now, the person who warned Pendergast that I was over here baking you pies had to be in town to tell him. Your boys weren't, but Jane Beal was."

"Keep talkin'," Jenner invited.

"Cimarron admitted to Jim that he was in town with Pendergast and rode straight here to get Forney. Does that add up to you yet?"

"Uh," Jenner said, and pawed his face out of shape.

"Let's pretend that Harlow and the others are Pendergast's men. I couldn't guess how they got here, unless Pendergast loaned them to you. Is that right?"

"He could have," Jenner said.

"Then can't you see how he's used you, and Jim? Mr. Jenner, he wants you and Jim Quartermain to kill each other!"

Rob Jenner packed and lighted his pipe, and champed on it. At last he said, "This part about Jane Beal—you making that up?"

"I'm guessing," Carrie said. "I can prove nothing."

"You'd like to do her in, wouldn't you? You're not tryin' to spare me. You want Jim Quartermain for yourself."

"Yes," Carrie admitted. "That's it. Not a pretty reason, is it?"

"But honest," Jenner said, "and that makes up for a lot of things." He looked steadily at her for a moment, then smiled. "Lass, you know that you're going to lose your man, don't you? He'll hate you for what you've said about the Beal girl, even if it's right."

"I know that," Carrie said softly. "Mr. Jenner, do you believe me?"

"No," he said. "But I don't disbelieve you either. This is somethin' a man'll have to figure out. You've explained some things to me, but there are questions yet unanswered."

"Ask me and I'll try to answer them for you," Carrie urged.

"What is the Beal girl getting out of this?"

"I don't know, "Carrie said. "Supposing Jim lost. You'd control the land then, except what Pendergast got out of it. That's something I can't figure out."

"I'd say that Jane Beal would have a good arguin' point in her favor, was you ever to accuse her of bein' in with Pendergast." Jenner shook his head. "You see why I can't believe it all? I'm sorry, lass."

"But if Jim wins—" Carrie began, then dropped it. "When I left the ranch house, I was so sure that I had it all figured out. I see now that I haven't. I'm sorry that things have to be this way, Mr. Jenner. I like you." She gave him a bold stare. "Why did you hang Gil Purvis? Did you hate us that much?"

He nodded. "I believe I did. Now I don't. An hour after it happened I didn't, but it was too late." He pulled his eyes away from hers and glanced at the flat valley. "Likely I'll have to meet Jim Quartermain over it. It's not a pleasant thought, because he's better with a gun than I am."

"He would talk to you," Carrie said. "I know he would."

Jenner disagreed with a shake of his head. "Purvis was his friend. He'll not let this go by."

"I'll talk to him," Carrie said. "Jim knows that no one can even up a thing like this once it's started. You've simply got to quit, and if you've been hurt worse than he has, you'll have to forget it."

"That's hard for a man to do sometimes," Jenner said.

"Will you talk to him? Please, just meet him and leave the guns at home."

"I'll not go to him," Rob Jenner said. "If he wants to come to me, I'll talk with him." He sighed and added, "You're a persuasive lass."

"Thank you, Mr. Jenner." Carrie slid off the porch and onto her horse. She saw Bushrod by the barn, and Winn Harlow came from the bunkhouse to stand in the doorway, watching her depart.

Once clear of the place, Carrie lost her confident air and began to worry. How could she explain to Jim Quartermain how she had managed to make Rob Jenner listen?

Quartermain would wonder. He would ask, and she knew that she was not very good at lying.

CHAPTER 14

Gil Purvis was buried beneath the cottonwood trees by the time Carrie Holderman returned to the Running W ranch house. Jim Quartermain sat on the front porch step where there was shade, a cigar firmly clamped between his teeth. He waited until she turned her horse into the barn, then stood up when she approached the porch.

Perspiration made her face slick and darkened the shirt across her shoulders and beneath the arms. She opened the top three buttons and fanned it away from her, then sat down.

"Did you go to Long Knife?"

"Yes, Jim. Are you very angry?" She tried to gauge the depth of his displeasure. "Jim, don't ride on Rob Jenner."

He took the cigar out of his mouth, and spun it into the dust. "What do you want me to do? Sit here? The crew is waiting, but they won't wait forever."

"Are you running this place or is the crew?"

"Purvis worked for this brand," Quartermain said. "He's got to be paid back. That's the law."

"The law of what?" Carrie asked. "Of men so proud that they'd rather stand off and kill each other before they walked a few steps and talked?"

Quartermain sat down beside her. "Carrie, what's the matter with you? I've never heard you talk like this before."

"I've never had a reason to before," she said, and mopped a sleeve across her face. "I'm licked, Jim. I've given up on you. Back in Crystal City I believed you wanted something different, a life where it wasn't kill or be killed. But now I don't think I saw you as you are. You're not trying to understand anything, Jim. You just want to hit Rob Jenner before he gets in another lick." She squinted at the shimmering flats, then looked up at the sky. Clouds were building up along the crest of the

127

mountains many miles away, cotton piled upon cotton with rain in the making. The heat was humid and sticky and her braids were damp from it.

"Because I was a woman, Rob listened to me. He promised there'd be no more shooting until you and he have a talk."

"Because you went to the trouble," Quartermain said, "I'll talk to him, but he has to come to me."

Carrie sighed and stood up. "He won't come to you. You have to go to him. Can't your pride stand that?"

"I'm not sure," Quartermain said, and went into the house. Jane was in the parlor, stretched out on the sofa. She wore a thin cotton dress and little else. Perspiration made it cling to her. She sat up and massaged her neck. "Damn this heat! Isn't there any let-up?"

"We'll get rain tonight." Quartermain slumped in a chair. "Right now I wish to hell Jenner's crew would ride in and get this over with."

"Maybe you'd better go to them," Jane suggested. "Cherokee was in a few minutes ago and he says the boys are getting impatient. They liked Purvis and they want to do something about it."

"They'll get themselves killed. Harlow and the Kid are professionals."

"Sometimes that no longer matters," Jane said. "If I was a man, I'd go."

"I guess you would," Quartermain said. "I'll go talk to Cherokee."

He wiped the sweat from his face and went out across the blistered yard. Jane got up and watched him from the window. She smiled with satisfaction until she saw Carrie Holderman sitting on the porch. Then the smile faded, for Carris was the one factor over which she had no control, the stabilizing force upon which Quartermain depended without knowing it.

Jane went to the front door and said, "Carrie, can you come in? I'd like to talk to you."

Carrie opened the screen door, after banging it once to remove the flies, and followed Jane into the parlor. The heat made Carrie's cheeks red and her shirt a damp, wrinkled mass that stuck to her annoyingly.

Choosing her words carefully, Jane Beal said, "I don't see any reason why we should go on like this, living under the same roof when only one of us has a right to be here."

"I'll help you pack," Carrie offered.

"I'm not packing," Jane said.

"Neither am I. We're stalemated, aren't we?"

"Not for long," Jane said. "Carrie, you don't know Jim like I do."

"That's what he's said. But then, I've never had the opportunities you've had." She smiled. "Jane, I'm not the kind of a woman who's going to hit a man over the head with his indiscretions. Did you think I was?"

"That depends on how indiscreet he was," Jane said. "Knowing Jim and his modesty, he probably left you with the idea that we were—quite casual." She laughed lightly. "As a matter of fact, he's not as mild as he seems."

"If you're trying to make some point," Carrie said, "get at it because it's too hot to beat around the bush."

"All right," Jane said. "Carrie, I could have created a scene when I came home and found you here, but I didn't want to embarrass Jim. I've left you alone and never said one word against you. You haven't played that fair with me. I don't like you. I've never pretended that I did. You see, I know your kind, Carrie—sweet face and honey words. I've had my share of trouble with them from time to time, but I've never worried about Jim taking them too seriously. You said you were leaving. Why don't you?"

"Now we're getting to the point," Carrie said. "What worked you up to it, Jane?" Carrie eyed her shrewdly. "I think you're getting worried about something. You're too anxious to get rid of me."

"I'll leave it up to Jim," Jane said. "He's out in the yard. Go ask him if he loves you. You don't have the nerve for it."

"I'm going to disappoint you," Carrie said, and left the room.

Quartermain was standing by the cook shack when Carrie left the house. He saw the stiff set of her shoulders and the hard way her boot heels hit, and he walked toward her, meeting her almost in the middle of the yard. Thunder began to rumble in the distance and a fresh wind came up suddenly, scuffing dust from the yard.

Near the bunkhouse men came out with rifles and belts

of ammunition. Carrie saw this and said, "So you're going to ride on the Jenners."

"Yes," he said. " I can't let this go, Carrie. Do you understand?"

"Better than you think. Jim, we've always given each other pretty straight answers, haven't we?"

"As straight as I could," he said.

"Then I must be pretty dumb, or hard to discourage or something," she said. "I've made a mistake that a lot of people make, thinking that they knew enough for both of us. Jane thinks I ought to leave, and you told me to go home. I'm finally getting the idea, but I want to ask you one thing just to make going easier. Did you *ever* love me, Jim?"

"I thought I did," he said. "Carrie, if I knew—" he closed his jaws with a snap. What could he tell her? That he was afraid he would disappoint her, not live up to her expectations of him? Couldn't she see that he was different from other men? That the gun made him different? "No," he said, "I can see now that I never loved you. It was a nice dream but nothing ever came of it."

Carrie reached the point where her pride could no longer sustain her and tears formed in her eyes. "Thank you for making it so easy. I should hate you, Jim."

"Then hate me if it'll make it easier for you."

She shook her head. "I'm just sorry that you had to come back here. I'm sorry that you won't be alive two years from now."

"Why won't I?" He took her by the shoulder but she slapped his hand aside.

"Go fight the Jenners. Kill them all. When you're through you can sit on your throne with your queen, and when another man comes close you can kill him too. But take a good look at Winn Harlow before you shoot him. That's what you're going to be like in a couple of years, a man with no future and no hope."

She pivoted on her heel and started to walk toward the house. But she broke into a run before she had taken fifteen steps.

The wind bore down with more force, raising a tawny cloud of dust from the flats, and the sound of it muffled Cherokee Nye's approach so that when Quartermain took

130

one step to follow her, Cherokee said, "I wouldn't do that, Jim. Let her go. She don't belong here."

Turning quickly, Quartermain snapped, "Suppose you mind your own damned business!"

The old man did not seem disturbed. "This is my business. Time's come for some straight talk, Jim." He took Quartermain's arm and they walked toward the barn, not pausing until they were on the sheltered side. "Seems that your trouble's mainly women. Never was bothered with 'em myself. Too ugly to draw 'em in the first place. Howsomever, since you got this mess on your hands, gettin' rid of one of 'em takes care of things nicely." He paused to roll a smoke. " 'Cause, gettin' the right one's the proposition that stumps a man."

"Why don't you get to the point?"

"The point is," Cherokee said, "that this ain't the country for that city-breed filly. She's sure a sweet thing. I like her. A mite bossy, but she makes sense most of the time, which is more'n you can say for women in general. She don't understand trouble, Jim, not range trouble. Don't guess she ever will." Cherokee paused, slyly. "Jane does, though. That gal sure understands a lot of things. Been watchin' her and she's pretty smart. Now most women would have thrown a fit to find another woman in their house, but not Jane. She knows what she's doin', that gal sure does. She figured you'd have a guilty conscience where she was concerned, and all she had to do was stand around where you could see her and let it do the work. Like I said, that Jane's had you on the run since she was thirteen. Had Izee and Andy eatin' out of her hand too. She's smart and she knows you so she played her cards careful. Looks like she's won, 'cause Carrie's leavin' and you're danglin'."

"Not any more," Quartermain said angrily. He started to move away, but Cherokee pulled him back.

"Hold on a second, Jim. You won't stop Carrie now."

"The hell I won't!"

"You won't because she don't want to be stopped." Cherokee shook his head. "Sure is a shame, because I liked her. I guess she's taken so much now that the truth wouldn't make no difference. The hurt's too deep to turn back and say that it's all gone."

The front door banged and Jane Beal came out leaning against the fresh wind as she crossed the yard. She almost reached the barn before she saw Cherokee and Quartermain and altered her course.

She looked at Quartermain and knew that his anger was deep and unquenchable. Immediately she placed the blame on Cherokee Nye. "You big-mouthed old fool!" She flicked her eyes to Quartermain. "Jim, don't hate me. I had to fight with the only weapons I had."

"I guess I'm in the way here," Cherokee said. He stalked over to the cook shack where several of the crew had gathered around the door.

Jane watched him until he passed beyond hearing, then said, "Jim, I'm wicked, I admit that, but I truly love you."

"I don't think you have any love in you," Quartermain said. "I just found out that Cherokee was right—you were always troubling my conscious. But you don't any more. I promised Izee Beal that I'd save this for you. I'll keep that promise, but when it's over I'm leaving."

"You don't mean that!"

"Wait and see," Quartermain told her, and hurried to the house. He went to Carrie Holderman's room and entered without knocking. He found Carrie packing her clothes in the last suitcase. She glanced around at him, but did not stop.

"You've come to tell me you've changed your mind," she said. "Sorry, Jim, but I'm not buying it." She straightened. "I'll never believe you until I see you change, and I'm sure now that you won't. You just can't bring yourself to lay that gun down, can you? It's too bad. A pity, almost."

He grabbed her roughly and held her so that she faced him. "Carrie, can't you see how it is with me? How long would I stay alive if I put it down?"

"Longer than you'll live with it. It's a matter of choice."

She tried to get away and he cupped his hand under her chin and kissed her. For a moment she fought him, pushing at his arms and face. Then suddenly gave in and embraced him fiercely. He released her and she whipped out of his arms. "I hate you, Jim. You make me weak. Now let me get out of here." She began to pack again. "You'll have Jane and where you're heading it's just as well. I don't think you'd want a woman who would cry over you." She snapped the suitcase shut. "Would you find my handbag for me, please?"

Quartermain went out and saw it on a small end table in the living room. He took it back to her and she tucked it under her arm without looking at it. She had carried her bags to the hallway and now she closed the door softly behind her.

"Would you carry them for me, please?"

"You trying to twist the knife?"

"Yes," she admitted. "I'm human too, Jim. I want to leave marks on you like she did."

Jane drove a fringe topped buggy to the front porch and came into the house. She saw Quartermain with Carrie's bags and said, "It'll be a miserable trip, with this rain coming on, but then I suppose you're glad to get away from here."

"The quicker the better," Carrie said, and walked past her to the buggy. Quartermain put her luggage in the back and drew a tarp over it. Jane came out in a long traveling cape and got in, lifting the reins immediately.

When she came to the edge of the yard she looked back and found Jim Quartermain still standing there. Slanting a glance at Carrie, Jane said, "I can't decide which he misses, you or me."

"Does it matter?"

"Not any more," Jane said. "Really, Carrie, this is best. Jim's not the man you want. He's too well known in his trade. He'd never settle down and that's what you'd want him to do." Her victory was near now and she became talkative, almost eager to explain away her motives. "He'll ride on Long Knife tonight and he'll win because he's the kind who wins. He'll end up ruling the San Saba, but it takes a strong man to do that, a man who will have to use his gun now and then. I did this for him, Carrie. A woman should do that for her man, guide him when he is unsure which way to go."

"I could only offer him security and a little happiness," Carrie said dully. "Pretty pale compared to what you have." She listened to the rattle of the rig for a moment and watched the rain march toward them from the distant hills. Finally she said, "But I think you're wrong, Jane. Jim has changed and he won't ride on Rob Jenner. They'll talk, and when they do, there won't be any more fight. They'll go to town and face Pendergast and then Jim will have what I wanted to give him—a place to live where

133

men didn't come after him with guns." She looked at Jane Beal with the deep pleasure of one who sees the enemy thwarted. "Then where will you be with your cheating and lies, Jane? Will he want you? I doubt it. I think I'll stay in town for a few days and wait. If Jim talks instead of fights, he's not going to want you and I'll be there, waiting for him. It's something for you to worry about, isn't it?"

Jane lashed the team with the reins and the buggy picked up speed. The sun was gone now and a grayness came into the day as the rain advanced across the flats in drenching sheets. A moment later it reached them, a few splattering drops at first, then a deluge that soon turned the road to mud and made traveling miserable.

In town, Jane paused at the hotel steps long enough for Carrie to dismount and the clerk to get her baggage from the boot. When Carrie went inside, Jane drove to the end of the street and parked around the corner by the bank. She used the back entrance and went directly to Horace Pendergast's office.

Pendergast took her wet traveling cape and hung it up, then poured her a small glass of brandy. "A miserable day to be out," he said.

"I think we could be in trouble," Jane said, and told him what had happened. "She's planted the seeds in Rob Jenner's mind and in Jim's. If they meet and talk, and then come here to see you—" She lifted her glass and let the rest speak for itself.

"Yes," Pendergast said, frowning worriedly. "That could be very awkward, couldn't it? Is this woman out of the way for good?"

"She won't go back," Jane said. "I've done some worrying about her because she had everything in her favor. Jim's not the same man who rode out with Lee and Ben Bickerstaff. He's quieter. He thinks before he starts shooting. Revenge doesn't interest him much anymore. You know he was with McKitrich when he was killed and it did something to Jim. Made him see something that none of us can see."

"I think I'd better handle this personally," Pendergast said. "Jane, you go to my home and stay there. I don't want you at Running W tonight." He opened a small closet and put on his coat and hat, draping a slicker over

134

his arm. He went out, spoke to the cashier and came back.

"Remember your promise that nothing will happen to Jim," Jane said. "Horace, I'm holding you to that."

"I'll not go back on it," he said. "I just want to stir up trouble to the point where no amount of talk will ever settle it."

"I want Jim unhurt," she repeated. "Horace, I've done what you wanted. Now do this for me or you'll be sorry. I worked my father, got him to tell me all the ranch affairs so I could pass them on to you. I gave you the inside information you needed and never failed you. Don't you fail me now."

"I won't." He opened the back door, letting the rain and wind blast him. He looked at Jane for a moment, then closed the door.

She sat quietly for a moment, then walked behind his desk, opening drawers with a woman's curiosity. She riffled papers, then paused when her fingers brushed the small .38 lying there. For a moment she pondered. Then she picked it up and slipped it inside the sleeve of her coat and went outside.

CHAPTER 15

Pendergast got his buggy from the livery stable and immediately drove out of town. Pendergast did not worry unnecessarily. With Cimarron dead and Trixie burned out, his contact with the budding range war was gone, but he decided that it didn't matter too much. The scales could be easily tipped now, and when he finished, nothing could stop the war.

Already the squatters were getting nervous. Four men had come to town to ask about their notes in the event Running W and Long Knife ran head-on into a fight.

The foul weather made the ride to Long Knife unpleasant, but Horace Pendergast could accept the unpleasant if it promised to shower direct profit upon him. He endured the hour-and-a-half drive in stony silence, his jaws working on a soggy cigar.

Driving into Rob Jenner's yard, he dismounted as Audie the Kid ran from the bunkhouse and took the team by the bits. "When the hell we goin' to get some action around here?" the Kid asked.

"Soon," Pendergast said. "Stick around. I'll probably need you."

"I'm not goin' any place," Audie said, and led the team away. Rob Jenner came to the porch and opened the door for Pendergast. Jenner's face was dark and unfriendly as Pendergast went into the parlor, slapping rain from his clothes. Over by the fire, Parker and Bushrod turned their heads to look at the banker.

"I want some words with you," Jenner said bluntly, and Pendergast fired up a dry cigar.

"I came here to talk," Pendergast said, sitting down. "I heard that Cimarron has been telling lies about me and I want to get that straightened out."

"It needs some straightening," Jenner said. He leaned against the wall, a man unfriendly in manner, yet controlled by a strict sense of fairness.

"Then I'll try to straighten it out," Pendergast said. "Cimarron was a thief. He came to me with a proposition once, but I kicked him out of my bank and he never came back. And that woman of Quartermain's, Carrie what's-her-name, is simply a troublemaker who's trying to get her man hooked any way she can. Her claim that I'm plotting against you is absurd. Jenner, I gave you a good crew of men to protect yourself. Is that the work of a man who's against you?"

"Don't seem like it," Rob Jenner conceded.

"Of course it isn't!" Pendergast snorted and banged the ash from the end of his cigar. "Jenner, you're not a fool. Can't you see that Carrie lied to you and to Quartermain, trying to get you two stirred up? Didn't she come over here, butter you up, then lead your son into a death trap?" He waved his hand. "I know, Cimarron did it, but she set it up."

"Quartermain shot Cimarron for it," Jenner said. "Explain that."

"Simple. He shot Cimarron because Cimarron stole from him, no other reason. The girl twisted it around to suit herself."

"You may have something there," Jenner said.

136

"Then she had the gall to come back," Pendergast pointed out. "I don't like any marks against me, so I'll give you some pretty damn good advice. Go to Quartermain, now, today. But take Winn Harlow and Audie the Kid with you. They're quick with a pistol and the minute Quartermain shows his murderous intent, there'll be some killing done."

Rob Jenner raised a hand and brushed his whiskered face. "That would settle it once and for all, wouldn't it? Was he to want peace, I'd have to believe the girl. But if he made a move toward war—"

"You'd be in a position to give him a fight he'd not recover from," Pendergast inserted. "Rob, I'd like to see peace at any price, but remember who Quartermain is—a trained gunfighter, a killer who will stop at nothing. Your own son, Parker, can tell you about McKitrich. The man was an accident looking for a place to happen. He was searching for another excuse to kill."

"By damn, I'll go!" Jenner said. "Parker, Bushrod, you stay here with Mr. Pendergast. I'll go saddle my horse."

He went outside, and a moment later Pendergast followed him, unmindful of the slanting rain. While Rob Jenner was in the barn, Pendergast went into the bunkhouse and motioned for Audie the Kid and Harlow.

"I've fixed it up for you," he said softly. "You're going with Rob Jenner to Quartermain's place, but see that he doesn't get there. Make sure it's close to Quartermain's property, then hurry back here and break the news to the boys. We'll ride on Running W by sunset."

"Got you," Harlow said, and gathered his gear. He and Audie the Kid went to the corral for horses and Pendergast stood in the shelter of the bunkhouse door as they rode from the yard. He smiled faintly and splashed across the muddy yard to the house. If a man must spend time, he ought to spend it pleasantly, in a house.

The buggy ride had reduced Carrie Holderman's clothes to a sodden ruin, so she sent the hotel clerk for three pails of hot water and a wooden tub. When these arrived she locked the door, stripped off her clothes and lounged in the water for almost an hour.

The rain pelted the window, distorting the light that seeped into the drab room. Finally she stood dripping and toweled herself dry before slipping into her faded robe. She could recall other times like this, when she had felt like crying and was stoutly determined not to.

Alone now, with no one to see her, she could admit that she loved Jim Quartermain, and would probably never stop loving him, because he was what she wanted. But she had pride and if he wanted her, he would have to come after her. She wondered if her pride would allow her to accept if he did.

Two people can hurt each other and forgive each other, but then the hurting gets out of hand and goes beyond the realm of forgiveness. Carrie supposed they had gone too far, accused each other too bitterly for either to swallow and forget.

"I'm a coward," she said to the four walls.

Another part of her mind denied this, telling her that she had more than enough reason, but she was too honest to believe it. You weren't woman enough to fight Jane Beal, she thought, and her shame grew.

There was a small stove in the room and she built a fire to drive out the damp chill. A few hours ago she had been roasting. A few hours ago she had been happy, secure in the knowledge that she was offering Jim Quartermain a solution to his troubles.

I never offered him enough, she accused herself. That's been my trouble. I wanted him to be what I wanted, but I never gave him anything.

She sniffed and decided that she was coming down with a cold.

"Just what I need now," she said, and searched for her purse. She saw it on the bed and picked it up, frowning. This wasn't her purse. Then she remembered that she had told Jim Quartermain to find it and he had picked up the wrong one by mistake.

Carrie had Jane Beal's purse.

This amused her. She laughed, and then on a sudden impulse she opened the purse and dumped it contents on the hotel bed. Carrie saw the packet of letters and pushed them away, but in doing so, she turned the packet over and saw the address in Jane's neat hand.

At the sight of Horace Pendergast's name, Carrie's attention sharpened. She ripped the string binding the letters. She read one carefully, then hurriedly spread them out and sorted them as to dates.

For an hour she read, now and then exclaiming in a shocked voice. When she finished she bundled them again and wrapped them carefully before throwing her robe on the bed and dressing. She had no underwear with legs and she shuddered as she wriggled into the cold, damp jeans and flannel shirt. She had packed a raincape in the bottom of her bag and she tore into it, scattering clothes on the bed, so great was her haste.

Dressed and with the letters tucked next to her stomach beneath the shirt, she went downstairs and to the stable at the end of the street. The hostler was asleep in a back-tilted chair and Carrie shook him.

"I want a horse than can run, mister."

The hostler sat up and looked her over. "Got a stud back there but I doubt you can ride him."

"If he has hair and four legs," Carire said, "I'll ride him. Put a saddle on him."

The hostler went into the stable and saddled a calico stud and led him out. Carrie mounted, tucked the rain-cape beneath her legs, then gigged the horse and ran him out of town.

Now you're going to do another foolish thing, she said to herself. Quartermain might thank her for presenting him with the evidence that would expose Jane Beal as a traitor who stood by while her father and brother were killed, but Quartermain would never love her for it.

A parting gift, she thought, but for me, not for him. I'm a small person, she admitted. I can't stand to lose and this way I'll go away smug and happy knowing I've beaten her, but I've given Jim nothing but pain.

She tucked her head down and bent over the horse's neck, letting the stud run.

Winn Harlow did not like to ride in the rain, but Rob Jenner did not seem to notice it at all. Harlow rode on Jenner's right side and Audie the Kid brought up the rear, a length behind. No one wanted to talk, and the rain made a steady drumming against the earth, and water began to run through the minute depressions crossing the flats.

Rain softened the felt of Jenner's old hat and poured from the brim to soak his face and beard. Occasionally he would raise his hand to wipe it from his face, but other than that, he paid no attention to it.

His heavy face was studious as he rode along and when he came near Quartermain's fence, he turned to Harlow and said, "Man, I have a question or two that needs answerin'."

"I'm not paid to know the answers," Harlow said. His face was healing and some semblance of the old handsomeness was returning now that the swelling had gone down. He shifted around in the saddle to look at Audie the Kid, then shifted back, saying nothing more.

"It's naggin' my mind," Jenner said, "just how Pendergast knew Quartermain's woman was here this mornin'."

"What difference does it make?" Harlow asked. "She's like Quartermain, a sneak when she wants to be."

"She never struck me like that," Jenner said. Carrie's blunt honesty had seemed to match his own and the thought that she might have lied troubled him. "No," he said flatly. "The girl was tellin' a straight story, by damn."

"What story?" Harlow said. Audie the Kid came up on the other side of the old man and rode even with him.

"That Pendergast is a crook!" Jenner said in his braying voice. "She thought the Beal girl was working with that banker and it stands up. The Beal girl hears what goes on at Running W and when Quartermain's woman came back early this mornin', she must have run to town to tell Pendergast. Then he came to see me."

Rob Jenner suddenly pulled his horse to a stop, making the other two half turn to face him.

"What's got into you?" Harlow asked. "You backin' out?"

"No," Jenner said, "but I've come far enough with you two. Go on back. I'll see Quartermain by myself."

"Stubborn old coot, ain't he?" Audie the Kid said. He leaned his crossed hands on the saddlehorn and waited.

"Don't get balky," Winn Harlow said. "The boss don't like it and neither do I."

Jenner shifted the reins and raised his hand to unbutton his slicker. "I'm wonderin' now," he thundered, "what your orders were. To kill me or Jim Quartermain."

"He's smart, ain't he?" Audie the Kid said and ripped the snaps open on his slicker. Jenner tried to get his hand

140

inside the folds to where his gun lay but Audie the Kid drew and fired from the hip.

The noise caused Jenner's horse to rear even as he fell from the saddle and the two men edged close to look at the man in the mud. Harlow pointed his gun at Rob Jenner but Audie the Kid said, "Put it away, I don't get paid to miss."

Across the flats, someone shouted. Harlow flipped his head toward Quartermain's fence line. The guards there were peering through the rain. Harlow said, "Let's go back and tell our story to Parker and Bushrod. Them damn fellows of Quartermain's killed the old man as we approached the fence."

"They sure did," Audie said, and turned his horse as Quartermain's crew mounted and began to ride toward them.

There was no chance of pursuit and Harlow knew it. He did not even worry about the possibility that some of Quartermain's men had recognized him. When he came back he would have nine guns behind him and it wouldn't matter.

Cord Butram reached Jenner first and he began to shout to the men still coming up, increasing their speed. The rain was heavier now and the wind whipped it across the grasslands, beating against the earth.

In the distance, Harlow and Audie the Kid were vague shapes which soon passed completely from sight. They rode fast, and in a short time they dashed into the Long Knife yard and flung off by the porch. Parker had heard them ride in and he met them on the porch.

"Where the hell's Pa?" he asked.

Harlow removed his hat before speaking. "We were approaching Quartermain's fence when his crew turned loose on us. The old man caught a slug clean, Parker. We couldn't pick him up even, the lead was whistlin' so bad."

Parker began to swear, a running stream of profanity that went on for three minutes without repeating himself. Then he wheeled toward the door and bellowed for his brother.

"Get Shallak and the crew together" he yelled. "Quartermain's killed the last Jenner he's ever goin' to kill. We're riding in five minutes!"

"Yes sir," Harlow said, and ran toward the bunkhouse.

Horace Pendergast came out to stand on the porch. Bushrod buckled on his pistol and Pendergast put his hand on Parker Jenner's thin shoulders.

"Son, let me tell you how sorry I am to hear this. Somehow, I feel that I've brought this on you."

"Ain't your fault," Parker said. "You done all you could to keep peace with that killin' bastard. I'll get him the same way I got Joel McKitrich. I ain't afraid of no gunslinger. I'm as fast as he is."

"Of course you are," Pendergast said. "Faster, probably. They use tricks to catch a man off guard. Quartermain's told me this himself."

"He won't trick me," Parker said, and left the porch as Audie came up with horses.

"Be dark in another hour and a half," Pendergast said. "You'll be safer to wait."

"I'm waitin' for nothin'," Parker said, and he wheeled his horse to storm out of the muddy yard with his crew strung out behind him.

Pendergast watched them leave, a pleased man who could puff his cigar in content while other men fought and died for him. He had to resist an almost overpowering urge to get paper and pencil and figure up the profits.

To pass the time he added them in his mind. Rob, Forney, both dead, and likely either Parker or Bushrod would die in the coming fight. In the event that the gods did not provide, Audie the Kid and Harlow would take care of it on the ride home. They had Shallak and Davis along to keep the Long Knife crew back, and once the Jenners were dead, the others would scatter.

On Quartermain's side of the ledger, there was Purvis gone, and Joel McKitrich, who would have made a fierce ally now that the Jenners had foolishly aroused him. Quartermain would be dead by dark, as well as Cherokee Nye, who felt a real loyalty to Running W. The crew were just drifters, and once the fight swung to the side of Long Knife, they would desert, leaving Horace Dobbs Pendergast the victor.

A token payment to Harlow and the others, Pendergast mused, and then rake in the profits. . . . He sighed and spun his cigar into a mud puddle, a pleased man.

From the direction of town, a buggy made a moving dark spot against the gray curtain of rain. Pendergast's

142

attention sharpened, then tapered off to relief when he recognized Jane Beal. The girl pulled into the yard and dismounted by the porch. She looked around at the vacant ranch buildings and said, "Horace, I can't go through with it!"

"You're too late," he said. "Parker and the crew are riding on Quartermain right now. By tonight it'll be all over."

"I don't trust you," she said. "Horace, I'm sorry, but I've changed my mind."

"This *is* funny," he said, but the light in his eyes said that he did not think it humorous at all. "What do you think you're doing, telling me you've changed your mind? There's not one damned thing you can do if Quartermain meets with an accident. Are you going to scream? Who'd believe you?"

She recoiled a step from this man she had never seen before. Ruthless as he had been, Pendergast had always talked smoothly. Now he reminded her of a wolf snarling over a freshly slain calf.

"Horace, I never lied about Jim. You knew I loved him. I only did this because of him. You know that."

"You did it for yourself," Pendergast said, and the look in his eyes frightened her, causing her to retreat off the porch. "I think I'd better keep you quiet until Harlow and the boys get back," he said. "Jane, you're scared, and when a woman gets scared, she'll do anything."

He followed her then, and Jane dashed around the buggy to keep away from him. "Please," she said. "You can have my share of the Jenner land. Just don't let anything happen to Jim. Please, Horace, I'm asking."

"The time for asking is over," he said. "Jane, I'm not going to hurt you. I just don't want you going to Running W now, you understand?"

When Pendergast began to stalk her she seized the buggy whip and lashed him across the face with it, leaving a bright red welt. Pendergast cursed and tried to grab her but she ran around the horses and into the house, slamming the front door as he mounted the porch in pursuit.

She bolted the front door and leaned against it while he pounded, trying to break it down. She heard Pendergast leave the front porch and knew that he would circle

143

the house and come in the back way. She did not have time enough to run and bolt the back door.

So she stood in the hall, crying, waiting. The back door banged open. Jane Beal slid her hand inside her coat sleeve and touched the cold butt of the .38 revolver. Pendergast came to the hall doorway and stopped. He said, "Jane, be sensible. In a few months you'll get over him, believe me."

"I don't believe you and I won't get over him," she said, sobbing. She started backing toward the front door and Pendergast matched her step for step.

"Jane, I'm warning you. I don't want to hurt you, but you're staying here."

She showed him the gun then, and his eyes grew round and careful.

"I don't want to shoot you," she said. "Don't come any closer."

He spread his hands and smiled, walking toward her steadily. "Jane, you couldn't murder a man in cold blood. You're not the kind. A little lying and cheating, maybe, but not murder."

"Please!" Her back came against the door and he closed with her suddenly. He tried to grab her wrist and missed and she tried to strike him in the face with the gun and succeeded only in cutting him across the bridge of the nose with the front sight.

His breathing was a loud panting in her face and rain had made his face slick. She struck him again with the gun but he took the blow on his neck and pinned her against the door with his bulk. He grabbed her arm then and twisted and the gun went off, the report muffled against his body. He staggered back. "You! You!" he said, then fell. Jane dropped the gun and watched as the banker's legs gave way and he sagged downward. Rain continued to rattle on the roof, a steady sound that filled the empty house. She stared at Pendergast. He just looked like a fat man resting in an awkward position, but she had killed him. Killed him. . . .

She shuddered. She felt sick. She stood there, weaving, fighting down waves of nausea. But the very sickness helped to block the horror out of her mind. Somehow she managed to stumble through the front door and climb into her buggy. She let the rain pelt her face, washing

144

everything away but her resolve. It took only a minute, really, and then she lashed the horse hard.

"I won't be in time," she said aloud, "but I've got to try."

CHAPTER 16

Carrie Holderman arrived at the Running W ranch house five minutes before Long Knife descended in howling fury. They struck the north edge of the yard, killed a man who tried to run from the barn to the bunkhouse, then fired a dozen shots into the ranch house and took cover in the cottonwood trees.

Quartermain was in the parlor with her, trying to get a hot drink down her to drive the chatters from her teeth, when Parker Jenner and his crew overran the place.

They reached the trees before Quartermain could fire a shot. He cautiously approached a window and looked into the yard. The dead man lay by the barn, but no one else was in sight. Cherokee and the remains of the crew were in the bunkhouse but they might as well have been in Chicago because the Long Knife crew closed off the yard with their rifles.

Quartermain went into the kitchen to bolt the door and upend the table against it. Then he killed the fire in the stove and moved this against the table, making a solid bulkhead against anyone who tried to break it down.

The fire in the parlor was going strong. He doused it with a bucket of water. Carrie huddled down against the wall, her shirt and jeans soaking wet. Quartermain went into his room and came out with a shirt and pair of his pants, then turned his back while she stripped to the skin, dried herself, and dressed.

The shooting had stopped, leaving only the monotonous rattle of rain. He said, "Harlow's an Indian. He'll wait until it gets dark."

"There's the crew at the fence," she said hopefully. "Jim, they'll come as soon as they hear the shooting."

"Too far away to hear in the rain," he said. "Besides, they're likely dead. Parker would hit them before he came on in just to keep them from coming up later."

"Oh," she said.

Someone opened the bunkhouse door, peeked around the corner, then whipped around as a rifle cracked. When the echo died, the man lay in the muddy yard and did not move.

Quartermain, watching this, knew that he was in a bad spot. Over in the cottonwood trees, Long Knife could cover the entire span of the front yard and there was no way to get out of the house and circle them. Circle with what? he asked himself. His men were pinned down in the bunkhouse. Any time now, someone would get the idea of throwing a rifle bullet through the thin walls and either killing sight unseen or driving them out where the shooting would be better.

He touched a match to a cigar and set his rifle against the window sill. Glancing at Carrie, he asked, "Why did you come back, Carrie?"

"Don't you know?"

"Not any more, I don't." He leaned his shoulder against the wall and watched her. The rain had plastered her hair tightly against her skull and the braids were sodden ropes that she rolled between the folds of a towel. "I guess I was always a little afraid of your world, Carrie, full of gentle people. Afraid I wouldn't fit." He laughed wryly. "I was like the little boy who was afraid to talk for fear he'd swear, then spoke one word and shocked everybody. There's no place for a gun in your world, Carrie, but because I am what I am, there was no place in mine without one."

"We were going to make a place together," she said, "where there was no need, weren't we? What happened, Jim? Where did the dream go?"

"Just gone," he said. "Blame it on Jane if it'll make you feel better. Blame it on me."

"That's no good," she said. "If the dream had been real enough nothing would have happened to it."

A shot tore through the silence and inside the bunkhouse a man yelled. Then quiet fell like a cape over the yard. Quartermain reared up for his look, then settled back.

146

"I keep thinking of McKitrich," he said. "How lost he was near the end. Tired and confused and trying so hard to hang on to something that never existed for him."

"Like you think it doesn't exist for you?"

He raised his eyes to her. "Why, yes, I guess that's it. It wouldn't last for us, Carrie. A few years, maybe. Then I'd go out like McKitrich did, trying to hang onto a damned shadow."

"I'm not like McKitrich's wife," Carrie said.

Someone yelled from the cottonwood grove. When Quartermain didn't answer, the man shouted again.

"Hey, gunfighter! You comin' out today?"

There was pleasure in Winn Harlow's voice, a gloating triumph that he no longer bothered to conceal.

Darkness was not far off now and there was no slack in the rain. Carrie Holderman tucked her hands inside the too large sleeves of his shirt and said, "Too bad we can't have a fire."

Someone left the shelter of the cottonwood trees and did not take two steps before a fusillade from the bunkhouse cut him down. This was followed by a wicked fire from the Long Knife crew which drove the men in the bunkhouse into a panic. One tried to bolt from the door. Long Knife shot him through the leg, but he managed to crawl around the corner of the building to safety.

Quartermain watched this from the window and his interest picked up. If that downed man was not too badly injured and used his head, he could break this deadlock. Harlow must have realized this also, for he dispatched two men to circle the house in the rear. Quartermain ran through the hallway and into the kitchen to cut them off.

He wiped a pane of glass from the back window with a circular motion of the rifle barrel and fired as the first man tried to make the woodshed. The bullet tagged the man and he went end over end as he fell. The other man snapped a shot at Quartermain that stripped wood from the window frame, then ducked back into cover as Quartermain's tardy shot missed.

There were no further attempts to break free of the cottonwoods. Harlow was pinned down as well as he pinned Quartermain down.

The house had begun to get dark. Quartermain went

back to the parlor. He sat down by Carrie and said, "Why did you come back? Won't you tell me?"

"No," she said. "I intended to tell you, but I've changed my mind. I don't want you to hate me, Jim."

"I'd never do that, Carrie."

"Yes," she said, "you would if I did this thing."

Harlow sent up another yell. "Quartermain! What about a talk?"

Quartermain threw the front window open. "Talk about what?"

"I got you on the hip."

"Let's see you do something about it!" Quartermain yelled back.

Suddenly a gun opened up from the back corner of the bunkhouse, and Quartermain knew that the wounded man had dragged himself completely around the building and was now pelting Long Knife from the oblique. Harlow's crew ducked to the other side of the trees to get away from this fire, but in doing so, exposed themselves to Quartermain's rifle. He sighted quickly, dropped one man, then watched complete confusion grip the Long Knife crew.

The men in the bunkhouse had taken advantage of this and three men boiled out, making the corner in safety. Harlow's cursing was like a whip for now the fight had turned and the grounds were no longer dominated by Long Knife.

The loggerhead had been broken and Running W was deploying now to carry the fight. Shallak and Davis left the cover of the trees as the last of the light faded. Quartermain tried to head them off by shooting through the rear window, but both men made the back porch.

With this advantage, they kept him to the front of the house while Harlow and Parker Jenner made another rush across the yard. Guns popped raggedly now, the flashes bright against the sooty night. Shallak and Davis began to batter at the back door while two of Jenner's crew tried to gain the front porch, only to be driven back by Jim Quartermain.

There was no sign of the Running W crew now, but, someone in the bunkhouse fired sporadically, keeping the yard clear. At the back of the house, Davis tried to get through the window, and the mistake cost him his life. Shallak, warned by Quartermain's shot, lay down against the base of the wall and listened to the others fight.

Using the darkness as cover, Parker and Bushrod succeeded in getting into the bunkhouse. Quartermain heard a flurry of shooting and then fire broke out as someone kicked over the stove, scattering hot coals onto the dry floor.

"Time to get out of here," Quartermain said, and pulled Carrie to her feet. He edged into the dark hall and opened the front door. There was some spasmodic shooting near the barn but it seemed to have little effect either way.

The bunkhouse was burning brightly now, the flames shooting long fingers into the rainy night. Someone ran across the muddy yard, slipping and falling twice, then carried away a pitchfork full of flaming hay.

Quartermain threw his rifle to his shoulder to drop the man, then realized that he must not draw fire with Carrie beside him. The man went into the barn and it caught immediately. The horses were turned loose and stampeded with rapid shooting. Then Harlow began to shout in a bull voice and the gunfire died off.

"Quartermain, can you hear me?"

For a heartbeat, Jim Quartermain wondered if this was a trick to get him to reveal his position, but when he heard the back door of the house splinter, knew that it wasn't. "On the porch! There's a woman here!"

"All right," Harlow yelled. He revealed himself then in the light of the burning bunkhouse and barn. He had Cherokee Nye as a prisoner. "I'll let the girl go!" Harlow promised. "But you got to throw down your gun!"

"Don't do it," Carrie said. "Jim, there's some way out of this."

"I won't wait!" Harlow yelled. "Give it up or we'll put the fire to the old man!"

"He's not fooling," Quartermain said. "All right! What about my crew?"

"We want you! They can go when you show yourself!"

The barn was beginning to collapse in a shower of sparks and men dashed back and forth across the muddy yard. Someone along the perimeter yelled and a buggy came on at a run, sliding to a stop fifteen yards from the porch.

"I might have known it," Carrie said as Jane Beal got down and ran toward the house.

"Somebody stop her!" Parker Jenner yelled, then hit a man who raised his rifle. "Not that way, you fool!"

Long Knife was rounding up the remainder of Quartermain's crew now, herding them into a huddle and relieving them of their guns. Jane came on the porch, saw Quartermain in the blackest shadows and threw her arms around his neck, crying uncontrollably.

Carrie said, "That's the first honest emotion I've seen you display."

Jane jumped away from Jim Quartermain and whirled toward Carrie. "What the devil are you doing here? I left you in town."

"I'm not a dog who's trained to stay put," Carrie said.

"Quartermain!" Harlow yelled again. "You haven't a chance now! Give up!"

Inside the house, Davis had succeeded in firing the kitchen. The glow of the mounting blaze came through the hall and front windows. Quartermain threw his rifle in the mud and stepped down from the porch. Jane yelled, "Jim, no! They'll kill you!"

Carrie dashed off the porch unnoticed, retrieved the rifle and wiped mud off it with her shirt sleeves. She held it across her breast and waited when Quartermain stopped twenty feet away. Harlow and Parker Jenner came forward with Cherokee Nye between them.

Harlow yelled, "Let the others go! We got our pigeons!"

Quartermain brushed his holstered Remington around to the back of his hip and hoped that in the darkness the firelight would not glint off the cartridges in the belt loops. He watched Winn Harlow and waited. He knew his man. As soon as there was no more danger, Harlow would kill him.

Audie the Kid came up then, the grin still twisting his face. He spoke to Harlow. "Shallak's dead as hell. So's three others."

"Fine," Harlow said, and turned his head to watch Quartermain's crew gather ropes to hunt down horses. These three men stood in a row facing Jim Quartermain, with Cherokee Nye, disarmed, among them. Harlow said, "Friend Jim, this is something I've wanted for a long time."

"Now the waiting's over," Quartermain said. Then he flipped his head around when Bushrod Jenner yelled loudly. He was along the fringe of light thrown by the burning barn and he appeared suddenly, a vague group of men behind him.

The Long Knife crew, instead of shooting at this new bunch, gathered around them, laughing and coming on at a slow walk.

"What the hell?" Winn Harlow said, and Parker left at a trot, his boots splashing mud.

Three of the men were mounted and Quartermain recognized his crew at the fence, but he could not account for their being alive. As they drew nearer and finally stopped, he saw that they were dragging a travois.

Suddenly Rob Jenner's bull voice split the night. He shouted, "Get them two sonsabitches!" And his finger pointed toward Harlow and Audie the Kid.

Audie the Kid's nerve broke. He tried to make a run for it, but Bushrod left his horse and both men rolled in the mud. Bushrod used his strength without mercy and then Audie the Kid shrieked once and a bone snapped. Bushrod stood up with the Kid's gun in his hand.

Quartermain steeled himself against the urge to glance that way. He knew that the moment he took his eyes off Harlow he'd be dead. Harlow was cool and now he had only one thing in mind. He swept his coat aside and drew his pistol. The man was fast and Quartermain's doctored .44 recoiled a scant shade before Harlow shot. Harlow staggered and planted his feet wide in the mud. A look of stunned surprise spread over his face and then he pitched forward, splashing mud over Quartermain's boots. Rob Jenner was bellowing in a bull voice and the remainder of Quartermain's crew went after Davis who came boldly to the front porch, expecting Harlow to have everything in hand.

Quartermain walked over to where Rob Jenner lay on the travois and said, "What is this, Rob?" Rain still fell, but more gently now, hissing against the embers of the burned barn and bunkhouse.

Jenner looked past Quartermain at the ranch house. Flames licked from the roof and along the back and the rear porch gave way. Jane Beal was coming across the yard now, Carrie right behind her, still carrying the rifle.

Jenner said, "Harlow and the Kid tried to kill me and blame it on you. Seems they convinced my boys of it." He smiled. "I was tryin' to get at my gun and the bullet broke my arm. Lucky, or it would have dusted me." He stopped talking when Jane came up to stand by Jim Quartermain. Rob Jenner asked, "What kind of a woman are you to betray your own people?"

"What's this old fool talking about?" Jane asked.

"He's talking about you," Carrie said evenly. "He wants to know how you could love money so much that you'd join Pendergast in a scheme to grab all of this for yourself."

"Damn you," Jane said. She tried to hit Carrie, but Quartermain blocked her and pushed her aside.

"Be careful now," he said, holding her wrist. "What proof have you of this, Rob?"

"Proof?" Jenner wrinkled his brow. "Pendergast came to me with a story of how you'd made a fool of me, you and her." He looked at Carrie. "Told me that this mornin' she'd lied to me, and like a fool, I believed it. He sent Harlow and the Kid with me and we was supposed to talk or make war with you, only there wasn't goin' to be any talk 'cause they had orders to kill me and leave me lay.

"I got to thinkin' and finally I remembered some supposin's that me'n your woman done this mornin'. We supposed that maybe Jane here was in with Pendergast. Now I didn't rightly see how this could be, but then Pendergast knew that your woman'd been to see me this mornin'. How'd he know that if Jane Beal didn't tell him?"

Parker and Bushrod waited, their faces dark and as stubborn as their father's. The Running W crew had gathered around, a close-packed circle. Some had tried to fight the fire, but the house was dry and fire gutted from within, so they gave it up.

Turning to Jane, Quartermain said, "All right, Jane. What have you got to say?"

"Are you going to believe *him*?" She sounded outraged.

"I asked you a question," Quartermain said. "I want an answer right now."

"Jim," she said, and touched him, "how can you think such a thing?" She saw no give in his face and said, "All right, I did mention it to Pendergast this noon. I was angry and he saw that so I said Carrie had gone to see Rob and we'd had a tiff over it. I told him she was leaving Running W." She looked around at the silent, wet faces, then shouted. "What are you staring at? Can I help it if a schemer turns simple conversation into—something terrible, like this?"

One of Jim Quartermain's riders spoke up. "Somethin' funny here, boss. We found Rob soon as he was hit—he wasn't more'n a half mile away—so we carted him way down to the other end where cookie had his wagon. Man ought to have shelter when he's hurt.

"We patched him the best we could, an' then I sent Britches over to Rob's place with the news that he was all right. There wasn't nobody there except Pendergast and he was dead as hell. Somebody'd shot him from up close. Britches had himself a look around and seen some buggy tracks that wasn't Pendergast's. The rain'd pretty well messed 'em up, but I'd say that rig over there made 'em."

He pointed to Jane Beal's buggy.

The eyes again focused on her and she wrung her hands. "All right, I was there too. Jim, you don't believe them, do you?" She wiped the rain from her face. "I got the idea from Carrie, making peace with Rob, so I stopped there on my way home. Pendergast was there and he acted like a crazy man. He wanted to keep me there, tried to hold me, and I ran into the house. I had a gun and I drew it to hold him off. He tried to take it from me and it —in the struggle it went off." She looked at each of them appealingly.

Carrie's voice was softly sarcastic. "You poor thing. You're trembling."

Jane's temper got the best of her. "Do I have to stand here and take her damned tongue?"

Quartermain's face was grave. Watching him, Carrie Holderman knew that he was weighing the evidence, and that his verdict was swaying toward Jane Beal. Finally he said, "Rob, I don't think you have anything conclusive."

"Of course he hasn't," Jane said. "He's just an old man who hates, and he's going to keep on hating until someone shoots him."

Carrie touched Jane Beal on the arm and said, "Are

153

you sure you and Mr. Pendergast never corresponded while you were back East?"

Surprise came into Jane's eyes, but the night hid it from all but Carrie. "That's ridiculous," she said. "Mr. Pendergast was a friend of my father's, nothing more."

Looking at Jim Quartermain, Carrie said, "Jim, you asked me twice what I came back here for and I wouldn't tell you. But now I will. When I was packing, I asked you to get my handbag, but you were confused and gave me Jane's." She unbuttoned her shirt and pulled out the letters. "She *has* written to Pendergast, Jim, many times, and all of these letters will show that she and Pendergast were in this together, all the way, except to the point where her own father and brother were killed."

Jane made a grab for the letters in Quartermain's hand, but he fended her away. He could not read them in the dark, but Carrie's voice carried the truth in it and he had no doubts now, no memories to sway his judgment.

"Give me my letters," Jane said, trying to reach around Quartermain. "Jim, I'm asking you to give them back and believe in me as I've always believed in you."

The men standing here were passing silent judgment and it bothered her. She had no support, no one who even cared to listen to her plea.

"Jim, I love you. That wasn't a lie." She pressed her hands together. "I'm everything they say, but never in that. That's why I went to Pendergast, Jim, to beg him not to have you killed. I wanted you above everything else. Don't you believe that?"

"No," he said simply, and let it go at that. He could upbraid her, accuse her of torturing his soul, taking it for her own purposes when she never had a right to his affection, but he left those things unsaid.

"This is your land," Rob Jenner said from the travois. "But you got to make a decision now. I leave it up to you."

Quartermain nodded and looked at Jane Beal. She was crying, the tears blending with the softly falling rain. "You have no home here," he said. "You have nothing coming. It's in my mind to take you to Brownwood to the sheriff, but that will get us nothing. Tomorrow I'll come to town and I'll have some papers for you to sign. You don't have to sign if you want to fight, but I'll tell you

154

this, Jane. I'll work the rest of my life to keep you from ever setting foot on Izee Beal's property."

There was no more for her here. She had placed the blue chips on the table, seen the cards fall and lost. Tears of defeat were not in her. She turned and splashed through the mud and got in her buggy to drive out.

When she had gone, Quartermain said, "Rob, we've got a mess on our hands. The bank will go into receivership until an auditor comes down from Brownwood. There might be some foreclosures on people around here, but we can co-sign that paper and keep them floating. Are you with me or against me?"

"Does this mean that you'll have your fence?"

"Fences and shorthorns," Quartermain said flatly. He stared at Parker Jenner. "Boy, you've got the burn in the palms of your hands and there won't be room for you on a range where men no longer carry a gun. There's a place in Arizona called Tombstone that's wide open. Get on your horse and go there where they have what you want."

Parker Jenner looked at his father. The old man said, "I'm tired of killin's, boy. Do what he says if you can't behave."

"Damn country's gettin' too tame for me," Parker said. He walked to his horse and the old man watched him mount up and ride out. There was regret on Rob Jenner's face, but he had made his concession to the changing times.

Rob sighed and said, "I'd be obliged if you'd cart me home, fellows. I hanker for my own bed." He touched Quartermain. "Your place is gone. Until you build again, I'd consider it kindly if you and your woman stayed with me."

"Likely I'll be over then," Quartermain said. He nodded to one of his men who mounted and pulled the travois out of the yard. Bushrod followed his father into the rainy night and Cherokee walked away, looking at the damage.

Carrie Holderman stood by Jim Quartermain. She said, "I hated to do that, Jim. I wanted you for my own, but not that way."

"Then why?"

"Because she'd gotten away with so much, Jim. All her

life she's gotten away with everything. She used you from the start, because she wanted to—what's the use? I just couldn't see her get away with this too. I'm sorry, I wasn't big enough."

"You've answered so many questions for me, Carrie," Quartermain said. "She had that way about her of makin' a man feel that he could never do enough for her, that she always had to have his affection." He laughed softly. "I never owed her anything, Carrie. All this time that I've been thinking I did, I didn't owe her one damn thing, did I?"

"No, Jim."

He looked around at the ranch, seeing the smoldering ruins, the stampeded horses gathering in the night near the gutted barn, but the sight did not sadden him too much.

"This is the price I have to pay for peace," Quartermain said. "I've got to start all over, from the bottom." He looked at Carrie then. "Do you start with me?"

"Yes, Jim. I'll always be with you."

"I have my place near Crystal City to sell," he said, mentally adding his assets. "That'll be enough cash to carry us and start another house. I'd like to build it away from the cottonwoods this time. Maybe nearer the road."

Cherokee Nye came up then, his boots sucking at the mud. He said, "She's a total loss, Jim, except for the cattle and fence. You're burned out."

"Only the buildings," Quartermain said. "We still got a crew?"

"Two dead and Acky's got a bullet in his leg. What do you want me to do? They can't sleep out in the rain now."

"We'll use Jenner's place until we build again," Quartermain said.

Cherokee grunted and thought this over. "That goin' to work? There was some bad feelin' between Runnin' W and Long Knife that ain't goin' to wash away with the rain."

"Sooner or later we'll have to learn to enter the same room without fighting," Quartermain stated. "Now's a good time to start."

"Uh," Cherokee said by way of agreement. "This country sure has been shot to hell in a hurry."

"It's been cleaned out," Quartermain corrected in the

156

mild voice he used when he wanted his undisputed way. "There'll be no more sidearms carried on Running W land, Cherokee. A saddle gun is all right, but no more pistols. Shooters aren't welcome here."

"I see," Cherokee said, and glanced at the Remington in Jim Quartermain's holster. "When's this startin'?"

"Now," Quartermain said. He lifted the gun. He turned it over several times and said, "Cherokee, a man worked on this for me to make it better than other men's guns, but it's all a lie. McKitrich had a set of Colts with no front sights and flat hammers and the actions had been smoothed to silk, but he died. No gun is better than another, Cherokee. They're all junk."

He pitched the pistol away from him and watched it hit in the mud. A timber inside the house parted and allowed one side to fall in. The fire had not completely carried through the parlor. Two walls remained, as well as half of the porch.

"See if you can find us a wagon," he said. "We'll take Acky to Jenner's and then send someone in for the doctor."

Cherokee walked away, a vague bobbing shape in the night. There was no more light from the burning buildings now, just the bed of sizzling coals that slowly went out beneath the sifting rain.

A break appeared in the clouds and a sliver of moon leered down on them.

Quartermain put his arm around Carrie and she came against him to share a meager warmth. He said, "You've got a lot to forget, Carrie. Can you do that?"

"Yes," she said. "It'll be no trouble at all."

He found that his cigars were ruined when he dipped his fingers in his shirt pocket, the rain having soaked through his coat. "McKitrich wanted it like this," he said, "but it never happened for him. He dreamed and saw nothing come of it. I don't want that, Carrie."

"It won't be like that, Jim," she said. "He wanted to change but he wanted to do it easy. It won't be easy." She smiled and stood on her tiptoes to kiss him. "He didn't have me either," she added and she was not bragging.

"No," Quartermain said, "he didn't."

Cherokee came back leading a team hitched to the spring wagon. Acky was in the back, lying on a pallet of dirty blankets. Quartermain helped Carrie to the wet

157

seat, then leaned over the sideboards and asked, "How is it goin' boy?"

Acky grinned past the set on his jaw. "Do me a favor, boss, and miss the bumps."

Quartermain climbed onto the seat and lifted the reins. "I like a smooth ride myself," he said, and clucked to the team. Carrie sat close to him, her arm around him and her head against his shoulder. They moved slowly across the flats toward the fence line. There was no hurry now. Tomorrow they would both begin to build, and in Quartermain's tired mind, tomorrow was as sure as his yesterdays had been uncertain.

Will Cook is the author of numerous outstanding Western novels as well as historical frontier fiction. He was born in Richmond, Indiana, but was raised by an aunt and uncle in Cambridge, Illinois. He joined the U.S. cavalry at the age of sixteen but was disillusioned because horses were being eliminated through mechanization. He transferred to the U.S. Army Air Force in which he served in the South Pacific during the Second World War. Cook turned to writing in 1951 and contributed a number of outstanding short stories to *Dime Western* and other pulp magazines as well as fiction for major smooth-paper magazines such as *The Saturday Evening Post*. It was in the *Post* that his best-known novel *Comanche Captives* was serialized. It was later filmed as *Two Rode Together* (Columbia, 1961) directed by John Ford and starring James Stewart and Richard Widmark. Sometimes in his short stories Cook would introduce characters that would later be featured in novels, such as Charlie Boomhauer who first appeared in *Lawmen Die Sudden* in *Big-Book Western* in 1953 and is later to be found in *Badman's Holiday* (1958) and *The Wind River Kid* (1958). Along with his steady productivity, Cook maintained an enviable quality. His novels range widely in time and place, from the Illinois frontier of 1811 to southwest Texas in 1905, but each is peopled with credible and interesting characters whose interactions form the backbone of the narrative. Most of his novels deal with more or less traditional Western themes—range wars, reformed outlaws, cattle rustling, Indian fighting—but there are also romantic novels such as *Sabrina Kane* (1956) and exercises in historical realism such as *Elizabeth, by Name* (1958). Indeed, his fiction is known for its strong heroines. Another common feature is Cook's compassion for his characters who must be able to survive in a wild and violent land. His protagonists made mistakes, hurt people they care for, and sometimes succumb to ignoble impulses, but this all provides an added dimension to the artistry of his work.